Becca took another step away from him and put her hands on her hips. "Did you just try to squash me with that big boulder?"

"Are you nuts? I just hired you to help me." Max eyed the massive boulder sitting at the base of the rock rise. "No rock that size has fallen around here since I've lived here."

"I saw someone up there. He tried to hit me with it."

"Get real," he said. "You haven't been here long enough to make any enemies. Unless someone followed you from the mainland." He saw her pale. "Are you here hiding out? Is that it?"

She flushed and looked away. "I don't have any enemies."

His suspicions rose. Why would a beautiful young woman—and she was the loveliest girl he'd seen in years—sequester herself clear out here? There was more to her story than she'd told him.

COLLEEN RHOADS

is a bestselling writer (as Colleen Coble) who loves to convey the compelling truth of God's love and grace through her fiction. Colleen has garnered a strong following in the Christian marketplace and many of her twenty-two books have appeared on the CBA Bestseller List. *Without a Trace,* Book One in her Rock Harbor series, was a RITA® Award finalist for 2004.

Windigo Twilight is the first book in her new series with Steeple Hill under her maiden name of Colleen Rhoads. Visit her Web site at www.colleencoble.com. She loves to hear from her readers! You can e-mail her at colleen@colleencoble.com.

WINDIGO
TWILIGHT
COLLEEN *R*HOADS

Steeple
Hill®

Published by Steeple Hill Books™

STEEPLE HILL BOOKS

Steeple
Hill®

ISBN 0-373-44219-X

WINDIGO TWILIGHT

Copyright © 2005 by Colleen Coble

www.SteepleHill.com

Printed in U.S.A.

Be on your guard; stand firm in the faith;
be men of courage; be strong.
—*1 Corinthians* 16:13

For my beloved grandparents,
Eileen and Everett Everroad,
who taught me about unconditional love.

Prologue

The sun threw a last golden glow across the horizon of Lake Superior. From her vantage point about five miles from Eagle Island, Suzanne Baxter could see nothing but the cold, clear waters of the big lake known as Gitchee Gumee.

She leaned against the railing of the forty-foot yacht and lifted her face to the breeze. Her husband, Mason, joined her.

"I'm glad we came," she said, turning to slip her arms around his still-trim body. Even at fifty-four, he could still make her heart race like a teenager's. They'd come through so much over the years.

He dropped a kiss on top of her head. "Me, too. It was time to make amends."

She bristled. "You mean let *them* make amends. *You* didn't do anything."

"Don't start," he said. "It was the right thing to do."

"I'm not so sure anyone but your mother feels that way. The rest stand to lose a lot of money with you back in your mother's good graces. She intends to leave you the lion's share now as her only living child." She pulled away and rubbed her arms.

"They'll get used to it." He swept his hand over the railing. "I can't believe we allowed ourselves to be gone from this for fifteen years. The kids should have been here every summer."

"We'll all come out in August. Jake will be done with his dig by mid-July, and Wynne's dive should be over about the same time. Becca will be out of school. I miss them."

"We'll be home by Wednesday. You could call Becca on the ship-to-shore phone. She should be around."

Suzanne hesitated. She'd like nothing better than to share things with her youngest child, but something still didn't feel right about the situation. She'd caught undercurrents at the old manor house, eddies of danger she wasn't about to share with her daughter yet. Becca would just worry. "I'll see her in a few days," she said.

He nodded and pulled her back against his chest as they watched the sun plunging into the water.

A rumble started under her feet, a vibration that made her toes feel tingly. It radiated up her calves. "What is that?" she asked Mason.

He frowned. His hand began to slide from her waist as he turned to check it out. But the rumble became a roar as the hull of the boat burst apart. The explosion tossed Suzanne into the air. As she hurtled toward the frigid Lake Superior water, her last regretful thought was of her children.

Chapter One

"I applied for a job on the island."

Waiting for a response from her siblings on the three-way conference call, Rebecca Baxter gripped her cordless phone until her fingers cramped. No telling how loud the opposition would be, though it was in her favor that her brother was in Montserrat and her sister in Argentina.

The answering hum in the line made her wonder if the conference call with her siblings had been disconnected. Then she heard Jake's long sigh and braced herself for his reaction.

"You're not going anywhere. The estate isn't settled yet, and you promised to do it," Jake said.

Her brother's reaction was surprisingly mild, but after twenty-five years, Becca knew he was maddest when he was quiet. She entwined her dolphin necklace—a birthday present from her parents—around her fingers.

"I had a phone interview this afternoon, and it went great. Not many people know about the Ojibwa culture and not many would be willing to go to a practically deserted island in the middle of Lake Superior. I'm pretty sure I'll get the job." Her voice didn't even tremble, and she gave herself a mental thumbs-up. She couldn't let them know how terrified she really was. This was the new Becca—strong and courageous.

"Jake, settle down." Her sister Wynne's soft voice was mellow enough to tame a Tyrannosaurus rex like Jake. As head of an archeological team, Jake sometimes forgot his sisters didn't have to jump at his command, not even Becca, the youngest.

"Don't encourage her!" This time there was no doubt about his displeasure.

Becca winced and held the phone out from her ear for a moment then put it back. She lifted her chin, even though no one but she knew it. "You can't stop me, Jake. Max Duncan seemed very impressed with my credentials." Even if he'd sounded as gruff as a grizzly bear. She grimaced and waited for the next objection.

"That was Cousin Laura's husband, right?" Wynne asked. "He's still there even though she's dead?"

"Yep. He's a writer. I found out he was researching a new novel set on an Ojibwa reservation and offered my expertise."

Jake snorted. "A perfect job for a career student like you. You've done some harebrained things in the past, but we're both too far away to bail you out of trouble this time."

"Jake," Wynne warned again.

"Okay, she just caught me off guard." His voice softened. "You seem so certain the explosion wasn't an accident. I'm not so sure, Becca. You don't have a shred of evidence."

Defensive hackles raised along Becca's back. Jake was a man of science who would scoff at the way she felt things. "I know it in my heart," she said quietly. "I'm not going to let them get away with it."

"I think it's just the way you're dealing with Mom and Dad's deaths. No one rigged the boat to blow. It was an accident."

Becca thought her brother's emphatic announcement was his way of convincing himself. She kept that opinion to herself. No sense in setting him off even more.

"Gram will recognize you," Wynne said.

It was Becca's main fear. "I applied as Becca Lynn and left off my last name altogether. I was ten the last time I saw her, and everyone was still calling me Becky. Besides, when I asked about the household, Max mentioned she was away on a trip to Europe. I've got four weeks to find out who killed them."

"Max and Laura had a little girl, didn't they?" Wynne's voice was thoughtful.

"Molly. She's five. She would have been only two when Laura died."

"There was some question that maybe Max had killed her, wasn't there? I don't like this, Becca." Wynne sounded worried.

Becca could picture her older sister clearly. She was likely sitting with both legs under her and twisting her long black hair around a finger. She missed Wynne with a sudden pang. The funeral a month ago had been a kaleidoscope of pain and disbelief where mourners and family moved through the landscape in a blur of pats and hugs. There had been no real time to grieve together.

No one from the island had come. The thought made

her scowl. Gram had outlived all three sons. The least she could have done was bid her last son farewell.

The lump in her throat grew until she wasn't sure she could speak. Becca sipped her licorice tea, cold now with a gray scum on top. The call-waiting beeped, and she glanced at it. "I have to go. Max is calling me back. I'll let you know when I get to Windigo Manor."

She clicked the button and answered the new call. "Becca Lynn."

"When can you come?" Max Duncan's deep voice asked.

"Immediately," she answered. As she made arrangements with him to be picked up at the boat dock, she wondered what she was getting herself in for. But she had to try.

Max Duncan laced his fingers together and leaned back in his chair. He was bored, no doubt about it. And just when he was beginning to think he might start writing again, a woman had called to see if he was looking for an assistant. If God cared about him, Max would have assumed He had orchestrated it.

No sense going there though. Laura's death had clearly shown him God didn't care about him. The realization brought an ache he thought he'd gotten over long ago.

He should move to the mainland, try to get on with his life. He'd been paralyzed since Laura's death and had allowed Lake Superior to exercise its cold charm in keeping him here.

If he'd relocated when Laura wanted to, she'd still be alive. He pushed the thought away. At least he was getting back to his writing. That was a first step.

He dropped the portable phone back onto his desk. The woman had said she'd come. She'd been evasive about how she'd heard he might be interested in an assistant—or even how she heard he lived out here—but he wasn't in a position to turn down badly needed help.

Maybe with her help, he could get this book jump-started. The front door slammed, and his daughter Molly flew into the room. Her face wet with tears, she hurtled into his arms.

"Whoa, what's wrong, sweetheart?" He cradled her as her wet cheek soaked the front of his shirt.

"The kids in town are mean!" She pulled away and scrubbed her cheeks with the back of her hand. "Audrey was whispering with Lucy, and I heard them say you killed Mommy. Why would they be so hateful?"

His daughter's precocious vocabulary and manner never failed to amaze him. Though only five, she talked and acted like a ten-year-old. It caused him to wonder whether he was depriving her of a normal childhood by forcing her to grow up among adults. He had heard the rumors—all of them. They failed to move him any longer, but he hated to see his daughter hurt.

"They're just words, Molly. Hold your head up high. We're still outsiders here, and people like to talk. They'll get tired of it if they see it doesn't bother you."

His daughter considered his words. "You mean they're just doing it to see me cry?"

"Yep."

"That's stupid."

"I know. So don't let them get to you."

She scrambled off his lap. "I won't. I love you, Daddy."

"I love you, too, baby girl." His heart ached as he watched her smile at him so trustingly. He'd cost her the mother who should still be here with her.

Chapter Two

Two days later, Becca found herself clinging desperately to the side of the boat as Lake Superior waves slapped the vessel like a giant hand. The motion left her feeling queasy. She'd forgotten how her stomach reacted in rough water. Lifting her face into the cold spray off the lake, she focused on the landscape instead of her tummy. Her cat, Misty, meowed pitifully from the cat carrier at her feet.

She watched the island draw nearer. Lake Superior glittered like some fabled jewel. She leaned forward and fastened her gaze on the imposing house just coming into view. A shiver started at her back. It had always been her first reaction. Jake used to say Windigo Manor looked like a great bird of prey looming over its hapless victims.

His comparison had given her nightmares when she was growing up. She told herself she was no longer a child, but the tremors wouldn't stop. She didn't want to think about the last time she'd been here. Staring at the manor, she watched it draw closer.

The house could have been the setting for *Jane Eyre*. Weathered stone and three stories high, its mullioned windows cast a glassy stare over the crashing waves below. She'd never felt comfortable in that house. That was probably the reason she'd never wanted to live there. And now, she was doing that very thing.

The sooner she found what she wanted and got out, the happier she'd be.

She rehearsed what to say to Max Duncan and smoothed her linen skirt with nervous fingers. The boat owner, Dutch, he called himself, eased the boat to the dock, then jumped out and looped a rope over a piling.

He shook his head as he looked at her. "If you don't mind me saying so, miss, you sure you know what you're doing, eh?" Dutch took off his faded baseball cap and scratched his head before slapping it back over his bald pate. "There's no fun times out here. The Baxters are a mighty dour folk. A woman as fine-looking as you could find another job with no problem."

He was a bona fide Yooper, as residents of Michigan's Upper Peninsula were called. Becca smiled at his characteristic twang, part Canadian and part Finnish inflection. "I'll be fine. You go on back." She straightened her jacket, then smoothed her hair. Max wouldn't be inclined to hire a woman who looked like a rattled mermaid.

She picked up the pet carrier, then clambered over the side of the boat, and planted her feet on the beach. The heels of her shoes sank into the sand, and she staggered. She bit her lip. She wanted to portray a persona of competence, not ineptitude.

Tugging her heel from the sand, she stared at the woods. She'd forgotten how the massive trees blocked out the sun. The wind soughed through the pine trees along the cliff's edge, and the back of her neck prickled as if someone were watching her.

She caught herself looking for shadows and laughed, though even to her ears, the laugh sounded shaky. Her grandparents' housekeeper, Moxie Jeffries, used to tell her all about the Windigo, Ojibwa spirits who roamed the North Woods looking for people to devour. Childish nonsense, surely. But why did her hands still tremble?

Dragging her luggage behind her with one hand, and carrying Misty's carrier with the other, she marched to the front door and lifted the knocker. The door opened, and Becca found her gaze traveling upwards to the dark blue eyes of the man filling the doorway. Unruly black hair spilled over a wide forehead that was creased in a surprised frown. His sheer size made Becca feel small and dainty which was something few men accomplished. At nearly six feet tall, she wasn't used to the sensation and wasn't sure she liked it.

It made her feel out of control. Not an unusual feeling, but Becca had hoped to be like Wynne, cool and calm.

She drew herself up to her full height. "Mr. Duncan?"

He nodded and leaned against the doorjamb. "Ms. Lynn, I presume?"

"Yes." She held out her hand. "Please, call me Becca since we're going to be working together." She wasn't sure she'd remember to answer if someone called her Ms. Lynn.

"You don't look like a Becca. I'd expect a Becca to be small and dainty, not a towering Valkyrie." His shoulders still blocked the doorway, and the surprise in his face changed to anger as he looked at the cat in the carrier.

Becca's mouth dropped open. She simply couldn't help herself. Didn't he know it was bad taste to remark on a woman's height? She bit her lip and told herself to stand up to him.

She recovered her composure and gave him what she hoped was a calm, competent smile. "Look, Mr. Duncan, I didn't come all this way to discuss my name— or my size. May I come in?" Though she hated to admit it, even to herself, this man's intimidating stare had shaken her. She just prayed he couldn't feel the fear radiating off her like heat baking off Eagle Rock in the summer. Some people could smell fear. She hoped he wasn't one of them.

His brows drew together. "Remember, this is a trial period only. I've never had a research assistant, and I'm not sure how I'll get along with one. Especially one who shows up with a cat without asking if it's all right."

The derision in his voice stung. He stared at her, his blue eyes raking her face like twin lasers. She wanted to cower but managed another smile. "Only curmudgeons don't like cats."

"Then I freely admit to being one. Just keep that animal out of my sight." He hesitated then took her suitcase and swung the door wide. "The parlor is on the right."

The words *I know* were on the tip of Becca's tongue, and she bit them back just in time. Whew, this was going to be harder than she'd thought. She started inside then tripped over the doorplate. Max grabbed her before she tumbled to the floor. She dropped the carrier and the door sprang open. Misty yowled and shot out across the hall and cowered under the hall tree.

Her face burned, and she tugged her arm out of his

grasp. "Thanks," she said, not wanting to look at him. She glanced around. It was exactly the same. Grandma's hall tree, its mirror scratched and the silver coming off in places, still graced the corner near the door. The same wallpaper brightened the plaster walls with a floral pattern. The faint scent of decay wafted in the air.

"Misty, come here." She tried to coax her cat out from under the table.

"Leave the stupid cat." Max walked past. "Let's talk."

Suppressing another shiver, she started down the hall. Without her grandmother's presence, the old mansion seemed even more sinister, especially with the man behind her in residence. He would have made a good pirate with his black hair and cynical smile.

Becca stepped inside the parlor and gasped at the wave of pain that swept over her at the empty room. She'd half expected to see her parents here, she realized. She hadn't understood how hard it would be to come here again and not see her mother bent over her photo scrapbooks and her father working on a crossword puzzle. Their presence had been like a safety net, and the sense of being on her own dried her mouth and made her knees tremble. She curled her fingers into fists, the sharp edges of her nails cutting into her palms. She couldn't afford to let Max Duncan suspect anything.

He set her suitcase down by the door and indicated the sofa. "Have a seat. Would you care for a cup of tea or a soda? We're not completely uncivilized here."

"No, thank you."

This time the smile was his, and Becca found herself scrutinizing him. She judged him to be in his midthirties, and there were lines etched around his mouth that reminded her of the pain he'd suffered with the loss of his wife, Becca's cousin Laura.

"Do I pass muster?" His sardonic tone broke her reverie.

Becca's face grew hot, and she looked away. "I'm eager to get to work. History is my passion, and I'm thankful for the opportunity to help you."

"I admit I'm leery of the whole thing, but it's time I got back to writing, and I don't have time for all the research. I hope it works out." He crossed one jean-clad leg over another. "I have a feeling you and I are going to mix about as well as sailors and society matrons."

Becca bit down on her angry words, her jaw aching from the effort to keep silent. If she'd had any other choice, she would have turned and stalked out the door. "I'll do my best to do my job and stay out of your way," she said in an even tone.

"The only thing I question is your sanity. Why would you be willing to bury yourself on this island? Running from a broken heart?" He said the last with a trace of mockery, and she stiffened.

"I like solitude. This place reminds me of the house my grandparents owned when I was a child."

"I think there's more than you're telling me." He rubbed his forehead. "I'm willing to give you a chance, though. Your pay is room and board plus a thousand dollars a month as we talked about on the phone. Does this still suit you?"

"It suits, Mr. Duncan. One other thing. I haven't set up a bank account yet, so if you could pay me in cash, that would make things easier."

"Fine, but call me Max." He rose and beckoned with

a crooked finger for her to follow him. "I'll introduce you to the housekeeper. She'll see to your needs."

Becca followed him down the hall to the kitchen. A short woman, almost as round as she was tall, was kneading dough on a rough wooden table. She looked to be about sixty, and her ample hips and stomach pressed against the flour-covered gingham dress she wore.

Moxie Jeffries. Becca had hoped she was gone by now. Her dour stories of her Ojibwa heritage legends had haunted Becca's dreams for years.

Her dark eyes narrowed when she saw Becca, and Becca had to force herself to meet the woman's gaze dispassionately. She prayed the housekeeper wouldn't recognize her.

"Moxie, this is my new research assistant, Becca Lynn. Becca, this is our housekeeper, Moxie Jeffries. Her brother Morgan is the groundskeeper."

Moxie Jeffries grunted and jerked her head. "If she can organize your notes, she's a miracle worker." Her dark eyes perused Becca's face. "You look familiar to me."

Panic tightened Becca's chest. She couldn't be recognized, not right from the start. "How strange," she said feebly.

Mrs. Jeffries shrugged. "It will come to me."

Becca could only pray it didn't. "I'm looking forward to my stay."

She offered her hand and almost winced at the woman's iron grip. A smug smile teased the corners of Mrs. Jeffries's mouth, and Becca realized the woman meant to hurt her with her crushing grip. Uneasy, she tugged her hand loose and turned to Max.

"I think it's time I got unpacked and ready for my duties." She wanted to get away from Mrs. Jeffries's suspicious stare. She doubted the woman recognized her, but it would be best to stay out of her way, just in case.

Max nodded. "Moxie will show you to your room. You can meet the rest of the group over dinner. They're all out on the boat this afternoon. I'm sure they'll be ecstatic at the relief from boredom your presence will bring—at least for a few hours. I'll bring up your suitcase in a few minutes."

A reprieve. Already exhausted, Becca followed the housekeeper, tripping over the first step. She hated being clumsy. If only she could be like her sister Wynne, small, dainty and graceful as a swan. Regaining her composure, she gripped the handrail to make sure she didn't stumble again.

She made a familiar turn at the top of the stairs then stared. Her eyes blurred with tears as Mrs. Jeffries stopped in front of the second door down. Becca's old room.

It seemed too good to be true she'd be housed in her childhood room. Becca moved slowly down the hall and stood in the doorway looking at the same space she'd occupied as a child. The wallpaper's yellow pattern had faded a bit more, but she'd forgotten the mellow tones of the oak casing around the windows and door. The books she'd read as a child occupied the small bookshelf under the window.

She stepped into the room. Ancient lace festooned the canopy bed, and she remembered lying here and studying the pattern in the lace. Her grandmother had made the canopy and coverlet for the bed when she was still a young bride, some fifty years ago. Becca touched the lace and let it drape through her fingers. The fine cotton felt soft.

Tears burned the back of her throat. The last time she'd been here, her mother had come in to pray with her before bed. Becca could almost imagine she could smell her mother's perfume here. Had Mom stayed in this room before the explosion?

She moved into a dapple of sunlight that warmed the oak floors. The Aubusson carpet under the bed looked different, but maybe she just didn't remember it. Becca bounced on the bed then kicked off her shoes.

"Anything else?"

Mrs. Jeffries's gruff voice startled Becca. She'd forgotten the housekeeper was still in the doorway. "No, thanks. I think I'll explore the house a bit, learn my way around."

The housekeeper shrugged. "Just stay out of the room at the end of the hall on the second floor. Mr. Max doesn't like anyone to disturb his wife's things." Her mouth in a tight line, she backed out of the room.

The room at the end of the hall. Though the warning was meant to keep her away, Becca knew sooner or later she'd have to check out that room. With the housekeeper gone, she stepped to the window and looked down onto the rocky shoreline. The lake looked blue and endless from here. The serenity was a lie. A month ago her parents had died in an explosion right off this point.

Her lips tightened. She would find out who killed them and make them pay. Her parents deserved it.

Chapter Three

Max wanted to send the woman packing. He knew it was irrational, but she made the hackles rise on his back. Besides, though she'd looked good on paper, she seemed too gauche and clumsy to make a good assistant. She'd likely spill coffee all over his papers and be too disorganized to be of much help. If he were smart, he'd go to her room right now and tell her he'd changed his mind.

He shook his head. The least he could do was to give her a chance. If he fired her now, he'd look like a fool. Besides, maybe she'd be good for Molly. For all her stiff manner and tailored suit, she'd seemed uncomfortable in her business attire, almost as if she was playing dress-up. The next few days should reveal the real Becca Lynn.

He'd wait and bide his time. Maybe whatever came through would prove a diversion for them all.

He went into the kitchen and grabbed a soda from the refrigerator.

"You shouldn't drink so much of that, Max," the housekeeper remarked. "All that sugar's bad for you."

"Keeps me sweet, Moxie," he said, popping the top.

She snorted. "I haven't seen any evidence of it mellowing you out."

"What's got you in such a sour mood?" he asked.

"I don't like you bringing in this new girl without asking Mrs. Baxter. You got no call to install a woman here without her approval."

"I'm not installing a woman here, Moxie! She's a research assistant, nothing more."

She raised one black eyebrow. "I saw the way you looked at her."

"You're seeing things. She's not my type at all. I like them short and round." He winked at her. "Like you. This one is too tall and clumsy."

Moxie sniffed but a smile tugged at the corners of her lips at his sly compliment. "So you say. But I'm not blind, even if you are."

Becca knew exactly where she wanted to go first. She found the attic door and opened it. The steps creaked as she went up to the third floor. She paused at the landing and listened. Dust motes tickled her nose, and she sneezed. She froze at a noise. It almost sounded like laughter. The hairs on the back of her neck stood at attention, and she held her breath.

The only sound that came to her straining ears was her heart thumping the blood through her veins. She was being a ninny. Being in this house again had spooked her. Gripping the rough wooden railing, she eased up the final flight of steps. Her head poked through the opening into the attic, and she blinked at the bright sunlight streaming through the mullioned windows.

The third floor had been her favorite spot as a child—at least until that last visit. Her heart hammered against her ribs, and she pushed away the memory. Easing up the last three steps, she stepped onto the rough, boarded floor and walked past stacks of boxes. Her gaze fixed on the door at the far end. Was it still there?

She realized she was holding her breath and exhaled. Her mouth went dry when her hand touched the doorknob into the end room. It had been fifteen years since she'd last stood here.

The doorknob turned noiselessly in her hand, and she pushed open the door. The laughter she'd heard came again, and Becca realized it was a child's laughter. She glanced around the room and saw a small girl crouched in front of the trunk that Becca had come here to find.

"Hello," Becca said.

The little girl whirled, the bonnet she wore slipping down her back. "Who are you? This is my place."

"You must be Molly." Becca smiled to reassure the child. "I'm Becca, your daddy's new research assistant."

Molly untied the bonnet from under her chin and placed it back into the chest. "You won't tell, will you? Daddy says I'm not supposed to come up here."

"Why not?"

"Daddy says old memories are bad for me. But I feel closer to Mommy up here. She used to play dress-up here, too."

Becca didn't answer but crouched beside the little girl. "Looks like you've found quite a treasure. It's fun to dress up and pretend to be someone else, isn't it? Who are you today?"

Molly's eyes brightened at the game. "I'm Priscilla

and I just came over on the *Mayflower.* You want to play?"

"I'd love to," Becca said. She rummaged through the chest, her fingers remembering the feel of the rich silks and brocades. She itched to pull out her favorite blue dress. It had belonged to her great-great-aunt, Mary Anne Baxter. The scent of lilacs wafted to her nose, and nostalgia took her in an almost painful grip.

She pushed away from the chest, her throat too full to speak. This had been a mistake. She stepped to the window and looked across Lake Superior. What was she doing here? It was ludicrous to think she could discover her parents' killer by herself. She'd never succeeded at anything in her life, and this was too important to mess up.

Molly leaned her arms on the windowsill beside Becca. "I saw a boat explode. Right there," Molly said, pointing. "It was scary and I cried."

Becca closed her eyes. She'd seen that horrific day over and over in her imagination. A lump formed in her throat, and she had to swallow three times before she found the voice to speak. "One of your daddy's boats?"

Molly's eyes filled with tears. "My auntie died on the boat. She was nice—my uncle, too. I wish they could come back from heaven. My Gram cried, too."

The lump in Becca's throat grew to gargantuan proportions. She felt hot and cold at the same time and suddenly claustrophobic.

"Your eyes are all red," Molly said, wiping her face. "You don't have to be sorry for me. My mommy had to go to heaven, too, so I'm used to it."

The little girl's precociousness took Becca aback. Molly talked practically like an adult.

"You don't talk much, do you?" Molly said, patting Becca's hand.

Becca managed a smile. "You talk enough for both of us. I'm sorry about your mommy. I'm sure you miss her very much."

"Daddy doesn't," Molly said, her smile dimming.

Becca's own smile faltered. Maybe the rumors were true about Max getting rid of Laura. "I'm sure he misses her, too," she said lamely.

Molly shook her head. "He said she was a witch. Is that like the Windigo? I didn't want to ask Daddy because his face scrunches up and he gets mad when I talk about her."

Right then and there Becca decided her first impression of Max was right on target. He was a bully and that was probably only the least of it. "Are you sure that's what your daddy said?"

Molly nodded. "I heard him talking to Uncle Nick."

At least he had enough sense not to speak ill of the child's mother to her face. Becca's ire cooled a bit. "He was probably just upset." She ran her hand over the little girl's hair, and Molly relaxed into the caress.

"Mommy used to braid my hair," she said. "Daddy's not very good at fixing it."

"You look pretty," Becca told her. "But anytime you need some help, you come to my room."

"You're nice," Molly said. "I hope you stay forever."

Becca's conscience smote her. Molly didn't deserve to get close to someone else and have them disappear. She should make sure to keep her distance from the little girl in the next few weeks.

She glanced at her watch. "Looks like we might have time to fix your hair before dinner. Go get your hair clips, then come to my room."

"Okay." Molly lowered her voice. "Just don't tell Daddy we were up here."

Even as she agreed to keep the little girl's secret, Becca wondered why Max objected to Molly's harmless excursions to the attic. Maybe there was something incriminating up here. She'd have to nose around.

Becca braided Molly's hair, then the little girl chattered away while Becca looked through the dresser drawers. Becca found herself wiping away tears when she smelled the lilac sachet among the linen. It brought back poignant memories of her childhood.

When six o'clock came, she was eager to meet the rest of the residents of Windigo Manor. One of them had killed her parents.

Unobserved for a few moments, Becca stood in the door to the dining room and felt the years slip away. The large dining room displayed an elegance she'd forgotten. A damask tablecloth covered the large, rectangular table, and real silver tableware lay at each place setting. A massive centerpiece of flowers graced the center, and a walnut cart laden with silver chafing dishes stood ready along the wall.

Her gaze lingered on a tall, dark-haired man. He had to be Nick Andrews, Max's half brother, though his mouth lacked the stern lines of his older brother's. His eyes held a hint of merriment Becca doubted she'd ever see on Max's face.

He turned and saw her. "You must be Becca, Max's new draft horse, though I must say you're much prettier than I expected."

At least he didn't remark on her height as his brother had. Becca smiled and stepped into the room, her hand reaching out to take his outstretched one. "You must be Nick."

"Right at the first guess. Must be the Andrews nose, eh?" He rubbed the bump on his nose.

"Quit fishing for a compliment," the woman next to him said.

About thirty, she had flaming red hair and the translucent skin of a true redhead. She offered a friendly smile that Becca responded to. "Shayna Baxter," the woman said, holding out her hand.

Tate's wife. Becca took her hand and smiled, then looked around for her cousin and finally saw him in the corner.

He hadn't changed much since they were children. Freckles still sprinkled his nose, and he looked at the world through good-natured dreamy eyes. Pouring himself a drink from the crystal decanter on the buffet, he turned and glanced at Becca. The curiosity in his glance didn't change, and she hoped he didn't recognize her.

"Welcome to our happy home," he said with a smile. "I'm Tate Baxter, and you've already met my wife. Just to orient you to the relationships, Max is my brother-in-law. His wife Laura was my sister."

"So we're all just one big happy family," Shayna said with a grimace that belied her words.

"I see you've met everyone," Max said from behind her.

Becca whirled to see him standing in the doorway. His dark, wavy hair looked wet, as though he'd just stepped from the shower. Dressed in khaki slacks and a red polo shirt, he looked good. She averted her eyes and reminded herself how deceptive good looks could be.

"There's my favorite niece," Tate said, smiling at Molly.

"I'm your only niece," Molly said, coming into the room to take his hand.

"But you'd still be my favorite if I had ten nieces," her uncle said.

Becca smiled. Tate had always had an engaging way about him, even when they were children. He'd been a favorite of their grandmother's, and probably still was.

"I want Becca to sit by me," Molly said.

Tate put his hand over his heart. "Spurned by the love of my life for another."

Molly giggled. "You can sit on my other side, Uncle Tate."

"A scrap thrown to the dogs," Tate groused. "I know where your true affection lies."

Molly looked uncertainly up at him. "I love you, Uncle Tate. You know I do. I just wanted to get to know Becca."

He grinned. "I was just kidding you, Molly. I know I'm your favorite uncle."

"I love Uncle Nick. too."

He put the back of his hand on his forehead. "Another arrow to the heart."

"Quit fooling around," Shayna said. "I'm famished."

Tate's bright countenance fell, and he took his place beside his wife without another word. Molly sat on his other side and patted the chair beside her.

Becca wondered at the tension between them. Maybe Tate wasn't as easy to live with as she imagined. She moved to take the seat the little girl indicated. Max followed her, and she stifled a frown. She wanted to talk to Molly and Tate without his intimidating presence.

Max seemed to sense nothing amiss as he settled into his chair and reached for the basket of hot yeast rolls. He took one then passed the basket to her.

Becca took out a roll then passed the basket on. She set the roll on her saucer and folded her hands in her lap. She wanted to pray for her meal, but everyone was looking at her, waiting for her to speak.

Heat rushed up her neck. She'd always prayed before meals, even in restaurants. For the first time, she was tempted just to butter her roll and dig in to her salad. She'd never realized peer pressure could be so great. Would God care if she prayed silently?

Though she knew God heard all prayer, audible or not, she realized the problem was her own attitude. Did she cave to pressure or stand up for God? She looked at her plate and took a deep breath.

"Do you mind if we pray before we eat?" she said.

Shayna's eyebrows went almost up to her fringe of bangs. A tinkle of laughter left her mouth. "I thought with Gram gone, we didn't have to deal with that nonsense. Looks like we have another little old lady with us, but in the guise of a young woman."

"I like to pray," Molly said. Her hand crept into Becca's.

Shayna grimaced and opened her mouth, but Tate put his hand on hers.

"That's enough, Shayna," he said. "Go ahead and pray, Becca. We're a bunch of heathens here, but a good influence wouldn't hurt us."

Becca knew he meant the words to be encouraging, but they felt condescending. He sat there with his liquor in his hand and a smile on his face that spoke volumes.

A hint of moisture burned the back of her eyes, and

she quickly lowered her head before anyone could notice. *"Thank you, Lord, for this food. Amen,"* she mumbled. Heat scorched her cheeks, and she kept her head down even while the silverware began to tinkle around her. Some witness she'd been. Her mother would have been ashamed of her.

She was going to have to do better than this if she expected to accomplish her goals here before her grandmother returned.

Molly squeezed her hand, and Becca raised her head. "Grammy will like you."

"I imagine she will," Max said on Becca's other side. "And we'll soon find out. She just called and she's heading home next week."

"Next week? I thought you said she'd be gone a month." Becca winced at the dismay in her voice and hoped no one had noticed.

Max nodded. "Yep. She's lonely for home. She would have come home tomorrow if she could have managed it."

A week. Becca's heart took a nosedive to her toes. That wasn't nearly enough time to find out who had murdered her parents.

Chapter Four

Becca punched her pillow for the umpteenth time and bunched it under her head. The sound of waves crashing on the rocks echoing through the screen on her open window should have lulled her to sleep hours ago. The breeze blew the gauzy curtains into streamers in the moonlight.

She'd been here two days without accomplishing a thing. She was going to have to pry harder. It went against her nature. She normally tried not to draw attention to herself. Her size was a big enough attention-getter. But this called for drastic measures.

She tried to pray, but the words wouldn't come. If she didn't discover who murdered her parents before her grandmother got back, her whole plan would come falling down around her ears. Dread soured her stomach. She'd never be able to pull the wool over Gram's eyes. She might be getting up there in years, but she'd always been observant. Mom and Dad had said she hadn't changed a bit.

If she failed to discover the murderer before her

grandmother got back, her only hope was to meet with her grandmother in private for the first time, and beg her to keep Becca's identity a secret. That was a long shot, and she knew it.

Becca sat up and drew her knees to her chest. She glanced at the clock on the bedside table. The glowing green numbers said twelve-ten. Maybe she could check out the room down the hall—Laura's room—then get a glass of warm milk. There was no way she could relax enough to go to sleep.

She slipped her feet into the slippers by her bed and grabbed her robe. Cinching it around her, she opened the door and stepped into the dark hall.

Tiptoeing down the hall, she put her hand on the doorknob to Laura's room. It was locked. She frowned then went to her room and got a bobby pin. Kneeling in front of the door, she was very conscious of every sound, every whisper of air movement from the furnace register behind her.

Maybe she should give it up. The lock resisted her prying and prodding, then finally, she heard a slight click. She turned the doorknob, and this time the door swung open. She stepped inside and shut the door behind her.

Reaching along the wall, she found the light switch and flipped it on. The soft glow from the overhead light illuminated a decidedly feminine room. She had to wonder how a very masculine Max had liked being in this room when Laura was alive.

A lace coverlet lay over a pink satin spread on the bed. More pink and lace festooned the windows. Lovely glass perfume bottles sat on a mirrored tray at the dresser. Even the bedside lamps dripped with lace.

Becca went to the closet and opened the door. All

Laura's clothes were still inside. She touched a red sweater. Laura's favorite color had been red.

Max must have loved her very much to have kept everything just as she'd left it. Becca surprised herself by feeling a touch of sympathy for her gruff boss.

"What are you doing in Mommy's room?" Molly stood in the doorway rubbing her eyes.

Becca whirled at the child's voice and put her hand to her throat. "You scared me out of five years of my life, Molly."

"Daddy doesn't like anyone to come in here."

"I was just looking around. We should get you back to bed. Let's keep this our secret, okay? Just like the attic?" Becca hated to feel she was blackmailing a child. "Never mind, you can tell your daddy if you want. I won't tell about the attic."

"I won't tell, either. I want you to stay and Daddy might make you leave if he knew you were here." Molly yawned and leaned against the door.

"Let's both go. I'm sorry if I was trespassing." She took Molly's hand and walked her down the hall to the child's bedroom. After tucking her into bed, Becca stood in the hall wondering what to do next.

From the top of the sweeping staircase, she heard the murmur of voices.

"Stay away from my wife."

Becca hardly recognized her cousin's voice. The venom in it didn't sound like Tate. She tiptoed down the steps. The argument seemed to be coming from the drawing room. She slipped into the dining room and stood in the doorway where she could hear. Her hand to her throat, she listened to see who he was talking to.

"I don't think I'm your problem." Max's voice was

even and measured. "You might check out your own attitude toward your wife."

"You've got a lot of room to talk," Tate spat. "Your own wife died trying to escape you."

"We're talking about your wife, not mine."

Becca's heart raced at the stress in Max's voice and she leaned in to hear better.

"Let's talk about your wife for a change. Everyone in this house has tiptoed around you for three years. You're no grieving widower anymore. Maybe we can be honest, man-to-man, for a change." Tate's voice prodded with laser precision.

"I'm going to bed. You've had too much to drink."

"That's always your way, isn't it, Max? The strong, silent type draws women like blackflies in June. But you couldn't keep your own wife from straying."

"You should know." Max's voice was tight. "You encouraged her."

"Is that what this is—payback time? I didn't think you had such passion in you." Tate's voice slurred. "It's no wonder my sister couldn't take your coldness."

"I'm not talking to you when you're like this."

Max's voice grew closer, and Becca looked frantically around for somewhere to hide. Heavy brocade curtains hung at the window, and she slipped behind them. Just in time, too, as Max stomped past where she'd stood moments before.

Becca held her breath, then his footsteps faded. She wanted to get back to her room, but she was afraid to move. Tate was still in the drawing room. She waited several minutes then peeked out. The dining room was empty, but she could still hear Tate muttering to himself in the drawing room.

She stepped from behind the curtains and raced up the steps, her inclination for warm milk forgotten. At the top of the steps, she turned to go to her room and encountered someone standing in the hall.

She uttered a shriek that was quickly stifled by a hard hand on her mouth.

"Shhh! You'll wake the house." Nick's breath whispered across her ear.

She relaxed in his grip. "You scared the life out of me," she whispered.

"Lots of people prowling around tonight." He took her arm and escorted her toward her room. "I wouldn't wander at night, if I were you."

"I couldn't sleep," she said. "I wanted some warm milk."

"Next time you want to wander, come get me and we can look at the moonlight together."

His voice was as warm as the milk she'd craved earlier, but it made her draw back. She wasn't used to a fast rush like that. Could he really find her that attractive? He had Max's good looks with none of the hard edges.

Becca pulled her hand out of his and pushed open the door to her room. "Thanks for making sure I made it back safely."

He smiled. "Next time we'll wander together."

Still smiling, she closed the door. It felt good to be admired like that. She tumbled into her bed and pulled the sheet up around her neck. Laura must have had an affair, with Tate's blessing. The hostility between Tate and Max seemed to be deep and hard to bridge. Did Gram know?

And did it have anything to do with her parents' deaths?

* * *

Molly sidled into Max's office, but he barely noticed as he glared at the first page of his novel. Bunk, pure hogwash. Panic played at the edge of his mind. What if his three-year hiatus from writing had destroyed his creativity? Maybe the muse had left him for all time. No editor would want this drivel. He shoved the keyboard away from him and ran his hand through his hair.

"Daddy?"

"What, sweetheart?" Maybe he should take up another profession. Carpentry, maybe.

"Daddy, when are you going to get married again?"

His head snapped up. "Where did that come from? I'm not getting married again, Molly. We're happy, just the two of us, aren't we?"

Molly angled her body against a round table by the window and played with the fringes on the crocheted doily on top of it. "Uh-huh. But it was nicer when there were three of us. And I can't have a baby brother or sister if you don't get married."

"You don't want to share me with a brother or sister anyway," he said with a smile. He held out his hand to her and she came to him.

"I wouldn't mind. I thought maybe Uncle Tate and Aunt Shayna would have a baby cousin for me, but they fight too much. That wouldn't be good. So we have to have one for ourselves."

Max tried to hide his amusement. "There aren't any women around to marry. They're all taken."

"There's Becca. She's nice."

Max's grin faded. "I don't think so, Molly. She's not my type."

"She's my type. She listens to me."

"I listen, don't I?"

Molly nodded. "But Becca is a girl."

"When have you talked to her enough to know you'd like her? She's only been here two days."

"I went to her room when she was looking through the drawers."

"What drawers?"

"In the dresser."

Why would she be going through the drawers? The lower ones in the guest room just had old memorabilia from Gram's grandkids.

"She was crying."

Max's scowl deepened, and all his earlier suspicions about why Becca would choose to hole up here came flooding back. She was hiding something. But what?

Becca brought down her packet of licorice tea from her bedroom and fixed a cup. She took her tea and an apple to the verandah and settled onto a chair there. This was her favorite spot in the entire estate. From here she could see the formal English garden her grandfather had built.

If she followed the path through the woods, it came out to another stone house, this one smaller and crumbling to ruin. The folly, Gram called it. It sat on a sheer cliff and looked out on the water from the other direction.

As a child, she'd loved to roam the ruins until the summer she fell and twisted her ankle during one such excursion. Her parents had forbidden her to venture there again, but she'd sometimes sneaked a short visit after her ankle had healed.

Maybe she'd just take a stroll through the folly after

breakfast. She glanced at her watch. And maybe not. It was almost time to get to work. She was relishing the research, even though Max usually only answered her questions in clipped tones.

She was determined to do a good job and show the maddening man she was capable and not some airhead as most people saw her. Mom always said a capable, organized woman lurked under Becca's surface flightiness, and it would come out in due time. Becca had decided it was time to prove her mother's prediction.

"Ready to get started?"

She whirled at the sound of Max's voice. "Now?"

He tapped his watch. "It's eight o'clock."

She gulped the last of her tea and stood. "Sorry, I lost track of the time."

He tossed her a steno pad. "I brought out a stack of books I've brought over from the mainland. You can start going through those today."

"I like reading." She fell into step beside him, and they walked to the library.

"I need to make sure I have myths and culture details exactly right. Did you bring me a copy of your thesis on Ojibwa culture? I've been forgetting to ask."

"Yep. I've got it in my room." This particular copy no longer had her last name anywhere on it.

Genuine pleasure lit his dark eyes, and Becca stared at the way his smile transformed his face. She blinked. Maybe he wasn't as dour as he appeared. No wonder Shayna found him attractive.

His smile faded, and he resumed his stride toward the library. Becca hurried to keep up.

"Put the copy on my desk by this afternoon."

No "please" or "may I," just a flat order. Becca's

warm feelings washed away. She gritted her teeth. "Say please?" she said in her sweetest tone.

He stopped again and turned, and this time she was too angry to notice. She plowed into his chest, and he caught her by the shoulders. The warmth of his hands seeped through her cotton top. She jerked away and rubbed her tingling arms.

His gaze probed her face, but she lifted her chin and stared him down. A smile tugged at his lips. "You've got spunk, Becca. I like that."

She struggled to keep her indignation, but his smile diffused her outrage. A smile tugged at her lips. "You're impossible. I'm more than happy to share my research, but can't you at least phrase it as a question?"

"You're right." He spread his fingers, palms up. "Let's start again this morning. I'm a little out of sorts, and I took it out on you."

That was as close to an apology as a man was likely to make, so Becca gave him one final glare then nodded. "Fine."

"May I read your research?"

He sounded almost humble, but his guileless smile didn't fool Becca. Max was a barracuda in bluegill scales. The next few weeks wouldn't be pleasant. But she'd worked for sharks before, and she could handle him.

"Since you asked so nicely, I'll get you a copy at lunch," she said. "Ready to get started?"

As she pored over the first of the twenty or so tomes at the desk, she found her gaze straying to where he sat at a corner desk. Pecking away on his laptop computer, he was managing to ignore her. She wished she could do the same to him.

She stretched and went to the coffeepot. "Want a cup?"

"Sure." He smiled and accepted the cup she offered.

"Is Molly close to her grandmother?"

"Very. Two peas in a pod. Molly can't wait for her to get home."

"Is she happy living here on the island?"

"She loves it, though I worry about her not having enough playmates. There are a few kids in town she plays with, but there's not much variety. I'm not sure what I'll do when school starts. Gram has offered to hire a governess, but I think she needs more interaction with other kids."

"She seems like an adult in a child's body," Becca agreed.

It appeared Molly was Gram's favorite these days. Had Becca's parents' arrival upset any expectations for inheritance? And if so, how far would Max go to protect his daughter's interests? His piratical good looks were in keeping with everything she suspected: murder, adultery—maybe even fleecing her grandmother.

As his assistant, she was in an excellent position to prove all she suspected. But not if her grandmother exposed her. She found it hard to focus on the dry research books in front of her with that worry hanging over her head. What would next week bring?

She sat back at her desk and pulled the book toward her then shoved it away and stood again. "I'm sorry, but I need a break. You mind if I take off for about an hour?"

Max's head bobbed slightly in acknowledgement, his gaze lingering on his computer screen. "Go ahead. Maybe you can get me your research while you're wandering around."

He obviously wasn't going to forget that. Becca nodded. "I think I'll take a walk and see if the fresh air clears my head."

"Stay away from the rocks on the south. The cliff edge crumbled some in the last storm. It's not safe right now." He bent back to his computer.

She nodded, though he was paying her no attention. Once outside in the bright sunshine, she felt she'd been released from prison. Her inner urgency to do something sprang to life, as well. Maybe a stroll through the folly would give her inspiration on how to approach her grandmother.

Taking a can of soda with her, Becca followed the brick pathway through the beds of daylilies and poppies, their bright flowers cheering her spirits immensely. Everywhere she turned, old memories resurrected. Keeping her cover from being blown was going to prove difficult.

The path through the woods was overgrown. Evidently no one wandered to the folly as she'd used to do. She pushed through the overgrown vegetation and fifteen minutes later stood behind the folly.

Cornish settlers had found their way here from the Keweenaw where they'd settled to work in the copper mines, and she was gazing upon the nineteenth-century ruins of a Cornish cottage. Three rooms still stood, but they had crumbled even more since she was here last. Wildflower sprigs poked through the rubble in spots, and she made her way to the perch where she used to watch the fishermen casting their nets offshore.

Settling onto a large piece of granite, she clasped her knees to her chest and grew still. The wind blew her hair around her head in a swirl, and she lifted her face into the sunshine. The scent of the water and the lullaby of the waves soothed her.

A sound other than that of the wind and waves penetrated her reverie. Like someone throwing stones. She cocked her head and listened. Dusting her hands on her jeans, she got up and followed the noise. It sounded as though it was down the grassy slope. A cave was this direction, if she remembered rightly.

Holding on to exposed tree roots, Becca slid down the incline and followed the sound. The waves reached for her when she got to the bottom. She avoided the cold spray and scrambled around the promontory edge of land.

The cave's opening was at eye height. She'd thought it so high up the slope when she was young. She could climb to it now if she wanted. Glancing around, she saw the footholds she could use. A sense of adventure quickened her breath. She'd always wanted to see inside. Setting her can of soda on the sand, she began the short climb toward the cave.

A pebble rattled past her cheek, then another. She glanced up in time to see a person's head vanish from view. Seconds later a boulder rumbled toward her, gathering speed as it came. She dove against the rock face and scrabbled the last few inches to the cave.

Just in time, she tumbled into the cave, shards of rock cutting her cheek. Debris rained past the opening then the boulder hurtled past, leaving a cloud of dust in its wake. Dazed from the near miss, Becca sat up and rubbed her stinging cheek. Her fingers came away bloody, and she stared at her fingers incredulously. She wiped her hand on her jeans.

She leaned out of the cave opening and looked down.

The boulder was big enough that she could slide out of the cave and stand on it without climbing down. Reaction set in, and Becca began to tremble. A few more seconds and she would have been lying squashed beneath the boulder.

Someone had just tried to kill her. This was no accident. She closed her eyes and struggled to remember the brief glimpse of the face she'd seen above her. Nothing came. She'd seen just a flash. It was there and gone so quickly she wasn't sure if it was a man or a woman.

Staring at the boulder, she decided it had to be a man. A woman would never have been able to shove that rock over the cliff. Even a man would have to be stronger than the norm.

The cave's cold began to seep into her bones, but she wasn't sure she wanted to climb down yet. What if the man was still up there? She glanced around the cave. The opening was large enough to allow sunlight to illuminate it to a depth of about ten feet. Darkness hid the rest.

Becca took a step farther into the cave, then another and another. Keeping her hand on the cave wall, she wished she had a flashlight. Who knew what kind of creepy-crawlies were back in here? The drip-drip of moisture came from somewhere, as well as the musty scent of stale water. The light from the opening grew dimmer, and she knew she should stop and turn around, but the thrill of the unknown kept her feet moving forward.

She came to a fork in the path. No way could she go any farther. Around the corner would be total darkness. Reluctantly, she began to retrace her steps. First chance she got, she'd come back with a flashlight.

She heard a sliding noise then what sounded like breathing. Her chest grew tight. Someone was in here with her. She froze, her breath loud in the silence. Just around the corner. Barely breathing, she bolted for the cave opening as a figure loomed before her, blocking her path.

Chapter Five

Tamping down his anger, Max stepped out to intercept Becca. He wanted to wring her neck. She had no business in this cave. It was off-limits to everyone. He couldn't believe no one had told her. He was going to have to.

She shrieked and beat at his face. He grabbed her by the shoulders. She fought like the Valkyrie he'd thought her when they first met and almost succeeded in breaking free of his grasp.

"It's just me," he growled.

She stomped her foot down on the instep of his foot with a man's strength.

"Ouch," he snapped, his grip loosening. "Are you nuts? I'm not going to hurt you."

She stiffened and pulled away. "Max? What are you doing here?" She squinted up at him as though unable to believe it was really him.

He bent over, rubbing his foot. "I decided I needed a break, as well. I was walking along the beach and heard a rockfall, then I saw your soda can by the water.

I was worried you'd been caught by the rocks. I'll know better than to think you need rescuing next time."

"Are you okay? Did I hurt you?"

He scowled at her helping hand, and she quickly withdrew it. "I'm just fine," he said through gritted teeth. "What are you doing here?"

"Exploring," she said.

"Exploring." He didn't bother to hide his disgust. "It's not safe to wander off by yourself in these caves."

"I know that. I turned around, obviously."

Narrowing her eyes, she stared at him with what he could have sworn was suspicion. What did she have to be suspicious about?

She took another step away from him and put her hands on her hips. "Did you just try to squash me with that big boulder?"

Had she hit her head? He glanced at her forehead, but the cave was too dim to see well. "Are you nuts? I just hired you to help me." Was the woman some kind of neurotic? That might explain why she was willing to come here to this remote island.

To his amazement, she smiled, the amusement stretching to her eyes.

"What's so funny?" He'd never understand women. Laura had been just as perplexing.

"I guess you wouldn't want to get rid of me already. I haven't even messed anything up yet."

"Are you planning to?"

"No, of course not." Her smile vanished, and she took a deep breath. "I was just scared. I'm fine now." Becca brushed the dirt from her jeans and started to clamber down to the sand.

"About as fine as a nor'easter about to blow," he muttered.

"Very funny," she snapped. She turned her back on him and scurried to the cave opening. Sitting on the edge of the opening, she half slid, half fell onto the boulder embedded in the sand. Easing off the rock into the shale, she started down the slope to the sand.

"Wait for me," Max called. "I'll help you down." He'd never met such an accident-prone woman.

She ignored him. Typical. His scowl deepened as he followed her out into the sunlight. Slipping and sliding, he made his way down the face of the rock to find her watching the waves roll in. She stood with her hands on her arms as though she was cold.

He eyed the massive boulder sitting at the base of the rock rise. "There hasn't been a rock that size fall around here since I've lived here," he said.

"I saw someone up there. He tried to hit me with it."

"And I'm the Pope," he said. "Get real. You haven't been here long enough to make any enemies. Unless someone followed you from the mainland." He saw her pale. "Are you here hiding out? Is that it?"

She flushed and looked away. "I don't have any enemies."

His suspicions rose. Why *would* a beautiful young woman—and she was the loveliest girl he'd seen in years—sequester herself clear out here on a minor project for little money? There was more to it.

"No enemies, huh?" He grabbed her hand "Come on, let's go take a look." She came with him unresistingly.

Max stooped to look at a depression in the rocks. "Here's where it was originally." He pointed to a rounded depression amid other smaller rocks and boulders. He went down on one knee and examined the area around the hole. What he saw nearly left him speechless.

He ran his fingers over scratches on a rock. "Looks like someone pried it loose. Look."

His suspicions rose even more when he looked at her face and saw the fear there. "Who do you think is after you?"

"No one." She shook her head violently. "It surely had to be a man to move something that big."

He shook his head. "Even a child can move a boulder if you've got the right fulcrum point on it." He glanced down the hill then turned back to her. "You said it was a murder attempt. You didn't just pull that out of a hat. Who is after you?"

She shook her head slowly. "I have no idea."

From the stubborn look on her face, he knew he wouldn't get any information out of her. "I have work to do," he said, taking her arm. "We'd better get to it."

Hurrying along beside Max, Becca didn't trust him. His appearing there seemed too coincidental. Her legs still felt shaky, but she managed to keep up with him as they moved toward the house. She wanted nothing more than a hot cup of tea and a chance to sit and reflect over what had just happened.

Mrs. Jeffries met them at the front door. "Mrs. Baxter telephoned. She's moved her arrival up a couple of days. She'll be here in three days."

Becca's legs went even weaker. How did she avoid bumping into her grandmother until she could schedule an appointment as the "new hire"? See her in person? Her stomach roiled in distress, and she licked dry lips.

"Good," Max told Mrs. Jeffries. "Would you fix a pot of tea? I think Becca could use one."

His perception pierced Becca's desperation, and she glanced up at him.

"You're pale," he said. "I think you should take the rest of the day off and rest."

Just what she needed. Maybe she could talk to the other residents and see what they all remembered of the night her parents' boat exploded. "Thank you," she said. "I am pretty rattled."

Nick Andrews was just stepping through the doorway and caught her final comment. "What's Max done now? He's always driving people away, but you have to remember he's a softy at heart."

His stepbrother sent him a quelling look. "I've done nothing to my assistant, and she's not going anywhere." His fingers pressed against Becca's elbow, and he moved her toward the chair by the window in the living room. "Mrs. Jeffries will bring you some tea. Have a seat, and I'll see you at dinner. You need some rest." His meaningful look failed to affect his brother who followed them toward the seating area.

Becca nodded and sank onto the overstuffed chair. The events of the past two days made her feel she was caught in the maelstrom of a whirlpool.

Nick lounged on a nearby chair with one leg thrown over the arm. Max glanced at him. "Keep an eye on her while I try to get some work done."

"That's a cushy job. She's easy on the eyes." Nick's grin made Becca's face heat.

Nick's grin was wide and infectious, and Becca

found herself smiling back at him. "Your brother can be a bit gruff," she said.

"A bit? That's like saying Lake Superior is a bit cold." He leaned over and grabbed the TV remote and flipped on the television.

"The two of you seem to get along well."

Nick grinned. "He's a great brother. A bit too anxious to run my life sometimes, but there's never any doubt it's because he cares."

"You're the youngest?"

Nick nodded. "Our mother left him and his father for my dad. To give Max credit, he could have resented me for that, but he never has, even when I disappoint him."

That explained a lot of Max's prickly manner. She couldn't help the niggle of sympathy for him. "How old was he when she left?"

"Five." Nick smiled. "Let's not talk about my brother. When are you going to go out to dinner with me?"

"Whenever you like." Getting out of the house and hearing what the townspeople had to say about the accident might be a good idea.

"How about Friday night? There's not much happening in town, but we can get a change of scenery."

"Sounds good." She began to relax. Mrs. Jeffries brought in the tea. Sipping the strong brew, Becca felt her buoyancy return. She could do this. She had to find her parents' killer.

"About seven?"

"Okay."

His grin widened, and he turned on a ball game and was soon engrossed in it. Swallowing the last of her tea, Becca stood. Nick was so caught up in the game, he didn't notice her leave the room. Becca wandered down the hall and out the back door. She heard voices in the garden.

Tate and Shayna were arguing on the terrace. Tate stood with his fists clenched at his side, his red face thrust forward like an angry rooster.

"You have no concept of money, Shayna!" He stepped back and ran his hand through his hair. "It doesn't grow on trees. You've got to watch what you spend."

"What else is there to do on this horrible island but shop? It's not like Wilson's carries anything but staples. I didn't get anything I didn't need." She stood and ran her hand along her husband's arm. "Don't be mad, Tate. It wasn't that much."

"Maybe today's wasn't, but what about the camera you bought online last week? It all adds up, Shayna."

Becca took a step back and looked for a place to escape. She twisted the doorknob behind her, but the door had locked.

Tate continued to rage. "It was nearly a thousand dollars. A thousand dollars we don't have, I might add." He turned and saw Becca standing by the door. His face flushed a dull red, and he gave a shaky laugh. "Uh, hello, Becca. I didn't see you there."

Becca wanted to sink through the floor. "Hi, Tate. I didn't mean to interrupt."

"We're done," Shayna said. "Tate has work to do."

"I sure do," Tate muttered, the anger in his face rearing again. "I have some calls to make." He went to the door, frowning when it wouldn't open. "Stupid latch is always doing that." He disappeared around the side of the house.

"Sorry you had to see that," Shayna said. She

stretched like the giant cat she put Becca in mind of with her red mane of hair and lithe limbs. The little-girl-lost expression in her face was at odds with the sophisticated woman Becca had first thought her.

"So what's to do around here?" Becca asked, sitting in the chair opposite Shayna.

"We can play croquet. Or go to town and browse through the fishing store. That's about it. I'm glad there's another woman here. We could play cards or a board game."

Neither sounded appealing to Becca, but Becca wasn't about to turn down the unexpected offer of friendship. She decided to tell Shayna what happened. "I think someone tried to kill me today," she said.

Shayna's cup of tea paused halfway to her mouth. "You're joking, right?" She put her cup back on the table.

"I wish I were. I was exploring the shoreline, and someone launched a boulder at me. If there hadn't been a cave to duck into, it would have gotten me."

"We get rockfalls here all the time. I'm sure it was an accident."

From the way Shayna was looking at her, Becca could tell the young woman thought her a bit neurotic. "Max showed up and looked at where the boulder came from. He said someone had pried at the boulder. He didn't think it was a natural rockfall. It was a much larger boulder than usual, he said."

"Pfooh, Max sees the dark in every bright cloud. I don't believe it for a minute. Maybe Max wanted to play the hero. You're an attractive woman."

Becca's own certainty began to crumble. Maybe she'd seen a flash of a bird or something. "I saw something at the top of the cliff before the boulder came crashing down."

Mrs. Jeffries came through the door with a tray of cookies as Becca spoke. Her eyes narrowed to slits. "It was the Windigo," she whispered. "I've heard him howling in the night. You must be careful. He is not to be toyed with."

Becca gave an involuntary shiver. "That's just a legend, Mrs. Jeffries."

"Most legends have their basis in fact," the housekeeper said. "Mind what I tell you, miss. Stay close to the house and don't go out at night." She plopped the cookies on the table and backed away, still looking frightened, then turned and bolted for the house.

Becca rubbed her arms. "I haven't heard that old legend in a long time."

"I'm surprised you've heard it at all." Shayna shuddered.

"Oh, it's one of those stories. The Windigo was supposed to be a huge creature with a giant head and big teeth, wasn't it? A demon who ate human flesh?"

Shayna nodded. "Sometimes he is said to wear a headdress and other times to have long, flowing hair. He is supposed to be half human and half beast."

Becca shuddered. "I'm glad it's just a legend."

Shayna grimaced. "Let's talk about something else. Imaginary cannibalistic creatures remind me of this island, anyway. It's eaten all the good times I used to have." She looked suddenly tired and defeated.

"We know it wasn't a Windigo who attacked me," Becca said.

"I say it was Max," Shayna said. Her green eyes sharpened like a cat eyeing a mouse. "Maybe he wanted to be the rescuer. He's been lonely since Laura died. You're the first eligible woman who's been here. All the women in the village are over fifty. The young ones take off for the mainland as soon as they can."

Could that be true? Becca hadn't seen any admiration in Max's eyes, but it could explain what had happened. And Max *was* there in time. "Maybe," she said doubtfully. She thought back to the argument she'd overheard between Max and Tate. "Are you good friends with Max?"

Shayna grimaced. "You've been listening to my husband." She stretched again. "I won't deny I think he's one of the most attractive men I've ever met. But I *am* married. And he's very conscious of the fact even though I might be persuaded to ignore that little incidental."

So Tate had reason to be jealous of Max. But was Shayna hiding their real relationship? Her eyes seemed guileless, and Becca longed to trust her. She needed a confidante.

"Put it all out of your mind," Shayna advised. "I'm sure it was an accident."

"There seem to be a lot of accidents around here," Becca said. "I heard about a boat explosion a few weeks ago just offshore. Were you here then?"

"Sure. I never go anywhere. Terrible thing. It was the old lady's long-lost son and daughter-in-law. They'd been estranged for years and had just reconciled."

"What was the estrangement about? From what I've heard of Mrs. Baxter, she's a sweet lady."

"Oh, she is. But she has a backbone of steel. I never heard what the initial spat was about, but she welcomed them with open arms when they arrived. She was devastated at their deaths. That's why she went to Europe.

But it sounds like even Paris couldn't comfort her. It would sure comfort me."

Gram hadn't been upset enough to attend the funeral. Becca felt the familiar pang of hurt. "What caused the boat to explode?"

Shayna shrugged. "I heard it was a leaky motor. I was right here on the terrace when the boat went off like a rocket. A spectacular sight, almost like the Fourth of July fireworks."

Becca tried not to flinch at her heartlessness, but she was sure her face had to betray some emotion. She glanced away. "You say it was Mrs. Baxter's son and daughter-in-law? That would make the man Tate's uncle?"

Shayna nodded. "He hadn't seen them in years, though. And I think he was a little miffed they showed up now because Gram started talking about changing her will. Mason was her only living child, and there would have been no money for any of the rest of us. Luckily, they died before she did it. The money is the only reason we hang around here all the time. Someday all this will belong to Tate."

Hearing it stated so baldly made Becca wince. Could Tate or Shayna have killed her parents? They stood to gain from the elimination of competition for the money. "Not Molly, too?"

"Oh, she'll get something, but Gram will want Tate to have the house and the lion's share." Shayna laughed. "Don't be so shocked. Why else would someone stay on this island with nothing to do? And Gram knows it."

"What about Max? Is that why he's here?"

"He could write anywhere. But as long as he makes sure Molly is close to Gram, he can be sure she'll get a share of the estate. And it's a big estate, I can tell you that."

Big enough to kill for? Becca snatched the words back before they left her lips. She couldn't believe that of Tate. He might drink too much, but he wasn't a killer.

Mrs. Jeffries came to the door. "Becca, you have a phone call."

"Coming." The only people who knew she was here were her siblings. She jogged to the door and took the portable phone the housekeeper handed her.

Shayna wagged her fingers at her and went inside. Carrying the phone, Becca went to the table and sat where she could see if anyone approached. She didn't want to be overheard.

"Hello," she said.

"How are things going?" Jake's deep voice came over the line.

Tears stung Becca's eyes at the sound of her brother's voice. She felt so alone here, isolated and vulnerable.

"Okay," she whispered.

"You don't sound okay," he said sharply. "What's wrong?"

She hesitated. If she told him what had happened this morning, he'd be on the first plane back to the States. "Nothing," she said finally. "I'm just emotional at being here where Mom and Dad died."

"Finding anything yet?"

"Just that practically everyone has a motive. Max wants his daughter Molly to inherit Gram's estate, Tate is hanging around to make sure he gets his share, and Mrs. Jeffries hates everyone."

"Sounds like a wonderful bunch of relatives," Jake

said with obvious disgust. "I think you should pack up and head home."

"Gram is coming back in a few days. She'll take one look at me and know who I am."

"So you won't have any choice. You can't stay there if everyone knows you're in line to inherit. Not if your theory is correct. I can't lose you, too."

"I'm hoping to talk to Gram alone and get her to go along with me for now."

"Fat chance of that from what I remember of her. She was a real stickler for telling the truth."

"But she won't have to lie, just keep quiet."

"Good luck. I don't see her going along with it."

Becca didn't want to talk about it anymore. It made her heart flutter in her chest. "How's the dig?"

"Great. We should be wrapping it up soon. I'll join you there once it's finished."

"Don't do that! You'll spoil everything. How would we explain you?"

"I could pretend to be your boyfriend or something."

"Ick. I don't think so."

There was a long pause. "Good point. I could just be your brother coming for a visit."

"Yeah, I guess that would work. We'll see how it goes. Have you heard from Wynne?"

"She called this morning. She's got a flight into Detroit in three weeks. We may both end up on your doorstep by this time next month."

Becca groaned. "I'd better work fast."

Chapter Six

Tate was swilling down a martini when Becca went inside. "Don't look at me like that," he muttered. "You Christians are all alike—out to suck the enjoyment out of life."

"And are you enjoying life?" Becca asked steadily. "You look like you're trying to drown your misery, but it's always there waiting for you when you sober up."

"A sermon. Just what I didn't need." He took another gulp of his drink. "Are you here for a reason or just to make me feel guilty?"

"I was looking for Max." Becca could see Tate was in no mood to listen to reason. The teasing man he'd been the night before as he joked with Molly was nowhere in evidence.

"His Highness is in his office slaving over his book."

"I thought you were going to do some work, too. Just what is it you do?" Becca wished she could reach her cousin. She remembered the carefree child he used to be.

"I have an online investments firm. That's about all

I can do holed away on this island." He put his empty glass on the buffet and grabbed the shaker.

Becca sighed. If she wanted to talk to him, she'd better do it now. He'd be drunk by dinnertime. "I was just talking with Shayna about the boat accident. Sad thing."

"Yes, it was."

Amazingly, she could see tears in his eyes. He seemed to have some feeling for her parents. Unless he was a good actor. In this place, nothing was certain.

"Did you know them well?"

"No, but it brought back bad memories of when my dad died. The second generation is all that's left of the Baxters. Us and Gram." He took a swig of his drink. "I don't want to talk about it." He turned so quickly, he sloshed his drink on the floor. Stumbling over the corner of the rug, he almost ran from the room.

Becca felt almost sorry for her cousin, though she couldn't figure out why he would be so emotional about an aunt and uncle he hadn't spent any time with. Maybe there was more to Tate than the shallow playboy facade he liked to project.

She mopped up his spill then went to Max's office. A grimace of concentration on his face, he sat at the computer typing furiously. Becca had never seen a man type so fast. The way he banged on the keyboard told her he probably went through one every few months.

"I'm bored," she told him. "I might as well work." Besides, she'd questioned everyone in the place except Max. This might be as good an opportunity as she got.

"Fine. You've got some color in your cheeks at least."

She sat at the desk and pulled a book toward her. "Where's Molly?" She picked up a fountain pen.

"That's mine." He leaned over and plucked it from her hand. "No one borrows my pen."

"Sorry. You didn't say where Molly was."

"At a sleepover with her best friend from town."

"I haven't been to town yet. What's there?" She had only dim memories of Turtle Town.

"Not much. A couple of run-down stores, five or six houses and a dock for the fishermen. A small school for the island children and two churches, though neither one pulls in enough parishioners to keep repairs done. Don't waste your time going there."

"It's clear on the other side of the island anyway, isn't it?"

He nodded. "And not worth the half hour's drive to get there."

He was going to a lot of trouble to convince her to stay away. Becca had to wonder if he was trying to hide something. "I might like to see it anyway. Want me to pick up Molly?"

"She's not due back until Monday morning, but sure. Knock yourself out. You can take my car. It's the town car in the barn."

"You don't seem the town-car sort," she blurted before she could stop herself.

He raised his eyebrows. "What sort would you expect me to drive?"

"Oh, maybe an old convertible you work on yourself."

"Like maybe the 1969 convertible in the other stall in the barn?"

She gaped. "You really have one?"

"Yep. The other was my wife's. I seldom drive it." His gaze mocked her.

"I see." She wouldn't look at him. Why did he always make her feel like a fool? She flipped open the book in front of her. "Did you get the copy of my research paper?"

"Yeah, I did. Looks well-written."

Heat spread up her chest at his praise. "Thanks. I worked on it forever."

"If I could just get this plot to come together in my mind, I'd be ready to write."

"It looked like you were writing when I came in."

He shook his head. "Stream-of-consciousness writing, trying to get a feel for my characters."

"It must be hard to think up new characters here when you are exposed to so few people. The visitors you had a few weeks ago must have seemed like a breath of fresh air."

He quirked an eyebrow. "Who have you been talking to—Shayna? They were quite ordinary people."

Becca bristled. "I wouldn't think a marine biologist would be ordinary. I love to talk to people with exotic professions."

"Science is boring to me. All those formulas to remember."

He was skirting her question, she realized. "So you didn't find them interesting?"

He shrugged. "Oh, sure, they were nice people. And Molly was excited to meet a new aunt and uncle."

"I bet they were quite taken with Molly." Becca turned away so he couldn't see the sorrow in her face. Her parents used to talk all the time about grandchildren. Now any grandchildren that came along would never know them. A lump formed in her throat, and she struggled not to cry.

"Yeah, they were. Molly still isn't over the explosion."

"She cried when she talked to me about it."

He frowned. "When did you talk to her about it?"

Too late she realized Molly hadn't wanted her father to know about going to the attic. "When I arrived. I ran into her." She prayed he didn't ask where.

His attention wasn't on her. He gazed through the window. "What's he doing here?" He jumped up and strode to the door into the side yard.

Becca looked out to see a man about forty tying his small boat to the pier. She followed Max out the door.

"I told you not to come around here." Max had his hands on his hips and barred the man's approach to the front door.

"You don't own this place. Not yet." The man had black hair with a shock of white running through it that hung over one eye. Slim almost to the point of emaciation, he didn't seem put off by Max's challenge.

"Gram isn't here."

That stopped the man. "Where is she?"

"That's none of your business. You've milked her for enough money."

The man's gaze drifted past Max and fastened on Becca's face. "Hello. Who are you?"

Something in his dark-eyed gaze put her at ease. He didn't seem at all threatening, so she couldn't figure out why Max was so antagonistic.

"I'm Becca. Becca Lynn."

"My assistant," Max said shortly. "And this is Robert Jeffries. He's just leaving."

"Bobby!" Mrs. Jeffries waved to him from the porch. "I didn't know you were coming."

Robert slipped past Max and kissed Mrs. Jeffries on her cheek. "Mom, you look as beautiful as ever."

Mrs. Jeffries fluttered her hands like a schoolgirl, and Becca gaped at the sight. The housekeeper had a girlish bloom to her cheeks, and she was smiling widely. Becca's gaze went back to Robert. She remembered him now as the suave, handsome young man she'd mooned over when she was a kid. She'd been much too young for him to notice, though.

"I just made some oatmeal cookies," his mother pronounced with obvious delight.

Tossing a look of triumph to Max, Robert sauntered after his mother.

Max practically growled as he stomped back to his office.

"Why don't you like him?" Becca asked.

"He's a sycophant, a man who uses women," Max snapped. He tossed a stack of computer printouts onto the desk and several fluttered to the floor. "He got Gram to finance his last harebrained scheme to the tune of ten thousand dollars which he promptly lost, of course."

Becca winced. "Still, what do you care? It's not your money. It sounds like Mrs. Baxter has plenty. Ten thousand dollars is probably nothing to her."

"Gram is too sweet and good for a jerk like that to take advantage of. She's like my own grandmother. Besides, I wouldn't let any friend fall under Robert's influence if I could help it."

He seemed to genuinely care about Gram, and Becca couldn't help but believe him. Maybe it wasn't all about the money for him, after all.

"I can't imagine why he's showing his face around here again," Max muttered.

"Maybe he just wants to see his mother." But even as she said the words, Becca remembered how Robert had frowned when he realized Gram wasn't here.

"I need to get rid of him before Gram comes home," Max said. "He's probably got some new scheme up his sleeve."

"Mrs. Baxter surely won't fall for it a second time."

"There's no telling with Gram. She's got a soft spot for lame ducks, no doubt about it."

Becca could only pray her grandmother had enough of a soft spot to help her when they met next week.

Dinner had been an excruciating affair. As soon as dessert was finished, Becca invited Shayna to her room. She could sense the other woman's loneliness and had decided she'd do what she could to befriend Shayna.

Shayna dropped to the carpet and began to look at the books on the shelves beside the bed. "Lots of classics here. I can't remember the last time I read a book. You seem fond of romances."

Becca's cheeks grew hot. "They're Christian romances," she said.

Shayna gave a sly grin. "Still looking for Mr. Right, huh? I suppose you won't consider a man unless he's a Christian, too?"

"That's the plan," Becca said. "A marriage is hard enough without trying to build a relationship where the husband and wife don't have similar beliefs."

"I guess that lets out Max and Nick."

Shayna's interest seemed a little too pointed. "I'm not really looking for a relationship right now. I've got plenty of time."

"I wish I'd taken a little longer myself."

"I've noticed you and Tate seem to be arguing a bit right now. Anything I can do to help?"

Shayna's smile faded. "I think we're beyond help." She stood. "Thanks for the female companionship. I needed a friend. I'd better go find Tate." She glanced at the books. "Mind if I borrow a book?"

"Help yourself."

Shayna selected a romance then hurried out the door. Becca could only hope the message in the book would make a difference. She prayed for her cousin and his wife then watched the sun sink over the horizon in a fiery display of red and gold from her bedroom window.

The house was quiet with her door closed. She wasn't sleepy though. Maybe she could go to the attic and poke around. No one would hear her. Anything was better than staring at these four walls.

She opened her door and listened. Voices echoed from downstairs. It sounded like Tate and Shayna, though they didn't seem to be arguing at least. Becca tiptoed along the thick rug in the hall to the door to the attic. She eased it open, and it creaked loudly. She froze, her blood pounding in her ears. What could she say if someone found her creeping up the stairs like some criminal?

The voices downstairs continued. She stepped onto the first attic step and pulled the door shut behind her. Darkness pressed in on her like a suffocating blanket. Her fingers fumbled for the switch and clicked it on. She breathed easier when light flooded the room above her head.

Treading softly, she went up the stairs to the landing above. The attic looked different without sunlight streaming in the windows. She didn't think she'd ever been up here at night before. It seemed smaller, more sinister. Maybe this was a bad idea.

Drawing in a breath, she told herself not to be a ninny. Another room, the door closed, lay beyond this one filled with boxes and Christmas decorations. She walked forward and pushed open the door. It was dark, and she heard a soft flutter. Her hand went to her throat, and she backed away.

And plowed into someone standing behind her. Becca uttered a shriek and jumped, whirling to face the person behind her.

"What are you doing up here?" Max didn't seem angry as he stood watching her. His head cocked to one side, he seemed genuinely puzzled.

"You scared the life out of me!" She took a deep breath, willing her heart rate to return to normal.

"You didn't answer my question." He crossed his arms over his chest.

Becca tried to laugh, but it came out shaky. "I was bored so I thought I'd explore. Is the attic off-limits?"

"No, but it's not the first place someone usually chooses to explore. Most women are afraid of the bats."

"Ba-bats?" She faltered. "I heard something in that room." She pointed to the room behind her.

He stepped past her and shut the door. "That's where they get in, so we keep the door closed."

She closed her eyes. "I hate bats," she whispered. "I had one stuck in my hair once." She shuddered at the memory of the last time she'd been here as a kid. She'd sworn never to come back up here, and now here she was.

A chittering sound came from the corner. Becca jerked around to peer into the shadows. Her hand went to her throat.

"Uh-oh, I think one might be in here," Max said.

Becca tried to run, but her legs seemed to be broken. Then a dark shape swooped from the ceiling in the corner and seemed to be coming straight at her head. She screamed and hit the ground. Her face pressed to the dusty carpet, she put her hands over her head then looked around for something to cover her hair.

She saw a discarded jacket on a chair nearby and scrabbled along the floor to grab it. As she flung it over her head, she caught a glimpse of Max snatching up a broken tennis racquet and turning to strike at the bat. She cowered back against the floor and listened to the sounds of battle.

Max was muttering under his breath, then Becca heard a *whop* and he uttered a grunt of satisfaction.

"You can come out now. The bat has been vanquished."

Becca cautiously lowered the jacket from her head. Max was grinning in a particularly revolting way.

"You think it's funny!" she accused.

His grin widened even more. He tossed the tennis racquet onto the floor and grasped her hand to pull her to her feet. "You're way bigger than the bat," he pointed out.

"But it's—it's icky," she said, still clinging to his hand.

He made no move to let go of her, either. And he was standing close enough she could smell his cologne, a particularly enticing scent. She knew she should move away, but he'd just saved her from a fate worse than death, and she couldn't deny her attraction to him. Her mind whispered that he might have tried to kill her this morning, but her heart didn't believe it.

His eyes darkened as his gaze collided with hers. He took a step closer, and his other hand touched her cheek. "Becca," he whispered. "Do you have any idea how beautiful you look standing there?"

Her heart felt as though it would beat right out of her chest. The tenderness in his fingertips seemed out of character for the gruff man she'd known the past two days.

"We—we should go down," she murmured huskily.

He drew in a deep breath, and his hand dropped away. "You're right." His voice seemed almost normal.

Becca wondered if she'd imagined the expression in his eyes. Maybe she was reading what she wanted to see. Most men were put off by her height. She'd lugged more boxes and suitcases by herself than she wanted to. A part of her yearned to be treated like a dainty flower of a woman.

Biting her lip hard enough to hurt, she pulled her hand free and went toward the stairs. "Thanks for saving me," she said.

"Any time," he said quietly.

Becca nearly ran down the steps. At the bottom of the stairs, she wrestled with the door. "It won't open." She banged her hand against it in frustration.

She heard Max's steps behind her, then his breath whispered across her cheek. "Let me."

She pressed her back against the wall so he could get to the latch.

"It doesn't have a lock on it, but it sticks sometimes."

He fiddled with it for what seemed like an eternity. His shoulders brushed her arm as he worked on the latch. Panic flared in her chest as she realized he could kill her up here, then stash her body. She told herself not to be silly, but she couldn't get over her suspicion of him.

He finally succeeded in getting the latch to open. The door swung open with a loud creak. "There you go," he said, but he still blocked her escape.

Her mouth was dry as she tried to ease by him. Her chest felt as if a seagull was trying to escape. "Th-thanks," she whispered.

He stood staring down at her, and she couldn't read the expression on his face. "Why were you really up there?" he asked. "I think there's more to Becca Lynn than I know. Maybe I should send you packing."

"I'm just an ordinary girl," she whispered.

He gave a bark of laughter. "You'd never be ordinary," he said. His fingers tucked a curl behind her left ear. "For my own safety, I should send you home." He stepped back. "But I don't think I'm going to do it."

Becca didn't pause to explain. She dashed past him as though the Windigo were on her tail. And for all she knew, that was just what Max was. A mysterious being who sucked the life out of others. Someone had done that to her parents. She just prayed Max wasn't that someone.

Chapter Seven

Becca tossed and turned all night. She awoke in a tangle of sweaty sheets with a dim sunrise casting shadows in the room. Her grandmother was coming home today. She felt hollow inside at the thought. God would have to work this one out. She couldn't do anything about it on her own.

She'd asked as many questions as she'd dared over the week she'd been here, but was no closer to discovering her parents' killer than on the day she arrived. Dinner on Friday with Nick had been postponed, so she'd found out nothing there.

The aroma of bacon and hash browns drifted up the stairs. Her tummy rumbled. Tossing back the covers, she decided she wouldn't worry about what the day would bring. Though she was no closer to solving the murder, she was here. Her grandmother wouldn't send her away. While it might be more dangerous if everyone knew who she was, she could still poke around.

Dressed in jeans and a long-sleeved cotton top, she went on sneakered feet down the stairs to the dining room. Max was the only one in the room when she stepped through the doorway. Her gaze collided with his, and she thought she saw a flare of some kind of emotion before he shut it off. Gladness, attraction? She wasn't sure what it had been.

"You look rested," he observed. "We have a lot of work ahead of us. Gram is supposed to arrive around one, so we'll try to cram a lot in this morning."

Mrs. Jeffries came into the room before Becca could do more than nod. Carrying a plate of bacon and bowls of scrambled eggs and hash browns, she didn't look at either of them.

"Something wrong, Mrs. Jeffries?" Becca asked when she saw the housekeeper's tight-lipped expression.

She shook her head without looking at them. As soon as she left the room, Max sighed.

"It's my fault," he admitted. "I tossed Robert out this morning. I found him going through Gram's desk."

She winced. "Any idea what he was after?"

"I'm not sure I want to know. He's always looking for a way to make a score."

"What did he say when you told him to leave?"

Max shrugged. "What could he say? I'm in charge with Gram gone. I escorted him off the premises."

"Why you and not Tate? He's her grandson," she pointed out.

"You can see the way Tate drinks and ask that?"

"Good point. Does he mind that Gram put you in charge?"

"Yeah, it's another bone of contention between the two of us. But he just has to deal."

"I wouldn't want to get on your bad side." Becca moved to the table and sat in her usual place.

"Be honest and you won't."

Was there a hidden warning in his words? She glanced at him from under her lashes. Maybe it was guilt that made her feel she had rocks in the pit of her stomach. She hated not being truthful in everything she did. It would all be out soon. Maybe sooner than she wanted. Would Max toss her out on her ear, too?

The rest of the family came in for breakfast, and she put her misgivings away.

Shayna sat beside Becca. "How was your day yesterday?" Becca asked her.

"Fine. I went shopping on the mainland and found a darling pair of shoes. Red ones. I love red shoes." Shayna spread her napkin on her lap and took a sip of coffee. "I miss Molly."

"I'm getting her shortly." Becca wondered if everyone expected more of the little girl because of her precocious manner and vocabulary. It was hard to remember she was a five-year-old girl at heart. She likely didn't have much chance at play since she was surrounded by adults all day long.

"Gram is coming home today, too," Shayna said. "You'll like her. She's never too busy to listen. That's about all there is to do here on this island—talk."

How well Becca remembered that trait in their grandmother. It was going to be hard not to kneel by Gram's chair and rest her head on her knees.

The sound of a motorboat drifted through the window. "Now who's here?" Max got up and looked out the window. "Gram is here already!"

Everyone got up from the table and rushed for the door. Becca felt as though she might throw up. How did she fade into the background until she could talk to Gram alone?

She backed away from the table and turned to creep up the steps. Max turned around in the doorway and saw her.

"Hey, Gram will want to meet you," he called. "Come with me and I'll introduce you."

Becca had no choice. She turned and went slowly to join Max. Praying her grandmother wouldn't recognize her right off, she tailed behind Max as he went to greet Gram.

Tate had run ahead and was hugging his grandmother as she stood on the dock waiting for the rest of the family to arrive.

Becca's gaze took in the new wrinkles on Gram's face, the hair that was completely white now instead of salt-and-pepper, and the added roundness of her short figure. Those blue eyes were just the same though—kind, gentle, but oh so discerning.

Becca knew she'd never pull it off.

She hung back, hoping her grandmother wouldn't notice her. Everyone was laughing and hugging Gram so Becca could watch undetected for now. She saw the grief etched in the wrinkles around Gram's eyes and the weary droop of her shoulders. She wanted to run forward and bury her face in her grandmother's bosom and grieve with her.

Her throat felt tight with unshed tears, and Becca struggled to control her expression. It wouldn't do for Gram to see her from a distance and wonder why some stranger was crying in the front yard.

In a lull left by Tate and Nick hauling Gram's luggage toward the house, Max looked back and saw Becca. "Oh, Gram, you haven't met my new research assistant yet." He held out his hand to Becca. When she stepped forward, he drew her to face Gram. "This is Becca Lynn. She just started a few days ago, but already her help has been invaluable."

Gram cocked her head to the side in a mannerism Becca now remembered so well. "Welcome to Windigo Manor, my dear." She took Becca's hand in her small one and pressed it. "You look familiar to me. Have we met?"

Becca's tongue felt glued to the top of her mouth. How could she lie to her own grandmother? God wouldn't like it. She swallowed hard. "I—I—" She broke off as shouts from the house interrupted her confession.

"Gram, phone call!" Tate yelled from the front porch. "I think it's Aunt Trudy."

Aunt Trudy. It had been years since Becca had heard that name, too. Gram's younger sister. Becca suddenly was overcome with nostalgia for the way life used to be when she was a child. Family around her, laughter and joy. Why couldn't life always be like that?

She had to tell her grandmother the truth when they next met.

The barn smelled of decades of old hay mingled with the faint scents of horse and engine oil. Becca found Laura's car easily enough under a yellowed tarp in the back. It didn't look as though it had been driven in a while. Surely someone had used it in the three years Laura had been gone?

She tossed the tarp back and got inside. It still smelled new, and she glanced at the odometer. Five thousand miles, hardly broken in.

The fawn leather interior was spotless, but a sense

of Laura still lingered in the car, a hint of perfume or something. Becca couldn't quite put her finger on it.

She shoved the key in the ignition and started the car. The sooner she got out of this car, the better she'd like it. It gave her the creeps, as though Laura wouldn't like it that Becca was driving her car. Stupid, she knew. There were no spirits lingering here. The Bible said it was appointed unto man once to die and after this the judgment. Laura had already stepped into eternity.

The old roads felt unfamiliar as she navigated the winding paths to the small town on the other side of the island. Her parents had often driven her to town on playdates or for groceries at the small general store that supplied the island with staples, but she recognized none of the landmarks. But then it had been fifteen years.

She passed a big barn on the edge of town with a sign that said Karola Farms and smiled. That was one building she remembered. Her best friend on the island had lived there. Saija Karola. Becca hadn't heard from her since the last time she was here. They'd never exchanged addresses, and once she and her family stopped coming to the island, memories of Saija joined the rest of the things she wasn't supposed to talk about.

She slowed the car as she entered the town. Village was more like it. It was more a place to slow down than to stop and browse. Six buildings comprised the village of Turtle Town. The general store, a gas station with pumps that had been installed in the late fifties, a sporting goods store, a restaurant/bar, a bank, and two churches. Most of the inhabitants were Ojibwa Indians.

Becca smiled at the sight of the old wooden church. She could come here on Sunday if Max let her borrow the car. Her gaze traveled to the restaurant. Bob's Eats looked as if it hadn't had a coat of paint in twenty years. The wood siding was gray and weather-beaten, and fly specks marred the plate-glass window.

The entire village had a sad, dispirited air, like an aging Ojibwa warrior too weak to put on war paint. Driving on through town, Becca stopped just past the incorporation sign at the yellow house on the right.

Its back to Superior's frigid waves, it looked like a house someone cared about. The yard was neat and well-tended and the paint fresh. Becca parked the car in the driveway and went to the door. As she neared the front steps, she could hear childish shrieks of laughter from inside.

She hoped it was Molly. The child was way too grown up and solemn for her years. Pressing the doorbell, she waited. Finally she heard steps and the door opened.

"Sorry, the baby was crying," the woman said breathlessly. The baby in her arms waved his tiny fists in the air and squalled louder. The woman plopped him over her shoulder, and he settled down with his thumb in his mouth.

"You do that so well," Becca said.

"Practice." The woman's gaze fastened on Becca's face. Her eyes widened. "Becky? Becky Baxter?"

The vague familiarity Becca had been feeling coalesced. "Saija?"

"Wow! I can't believe it's you." With her free hand, Saija tugged her inside. "I had no idea you were back on the island! I'm so sorry about your parents."

Becca glanced toward the girls playing a game on the floor. "Shhh, no one knows who I am," she whispered.

Saija frowned. "Let's have some coffee and you can tell me all about it." She led the way to the kitchen, a cheery room painted yellow and lined with blue pottery.

"Now give," she said.

Becca told her how she'd come back to the island. It felt good to spill the whole story, especially to Saija who had been a good listener even as a child.

"Whatever the reason, I'm glad you're back," Saija said. "If you get in trouble out there, you can always come stay with me and see what you can find."

"I hope I can keep this up awhile longer. Just don't tell anyone you saw me."

"My lips are sealed. Now how about some coffee and cookies?"

Food had been Saija's solution even when they were children, and Becca smiled and took a warm cookie. It was good to be back.

Becca took Molly back to Windigo Manor, then spent the entire afternoon on tenterhooks in the office. It was all she could do to keep her notes coherent. The call came just before the dinner hour. Gram wanted to see her.

Standing outside her grandmother's sitting room, she took a deep breath and rapped on the door.

"Come in, dear."

Her stomach dropped to her toes at the soft voice. She opened the door and stepped inside.

Her grandmother was in a chair by the window. The sunlight illuminated her soft white curls. "Come here, Becky," Gram said firmly. "And tell me why you're here under false pretenses."

Becca's shoulders sagged. "When did you know?" she whispered, moving forward on the thick carpet.

"As soon as I rested a bit." She held out her arms, and her face contorted. Tears made her blue eyes look large and luminous. "Come here so I can hold you."

Becca dropped to her knees by the chair and fell into her grandmother's arms. It was like coming home. She smelled the sweet vanilla scent of Gram's body spray, felt the softness of her arms and body. In her mind, she was a little girl again listening to tales of Brer Rabbit.

She sobbed against her grandmother's chest while Gram cried in her hair. Finally her grandmother pulled away and put her palms on either side of Becca's face. "Little Becky, all grown up." She smoothed the curls back from Becca's face. "I've missed so much of your growing-up years. They can never come again." Tears welled again, but she made an obvious effort to control them.

"I'm sorry, Gram," Becca whispered.

"You're here now." Her grandmother kept possession of Becca's hand but leaned back in her chair. "Now tell me what's going on."

"I think Mom and Dad were murdered," Becca said.

Her grandmother's face went white, and her fingers tightened on Becca's. "I don't want to believe that," she said slowly.

Becca squeezed her eyes shut. "I know," she choked out. She opened her eyes and stared into her grandmother's face. "I just know it, Gram. I came to find out who might have wanted to kill them. And why they left here when I was ten and never came to see you again."

Gram bit her lip, her gaze straying to the window. "It's hard to talk about."

"You reconciled when they were here, right?"

"Of course. As soon as I saw your father, we hugged

and cried much as you and I are doing now. It was as if the years fell away in a moment."

"What was the argument about?" Becca persisted.

"Foolishness." Gram sighed and relinquished Becca's hand. She stood and went to the window, looking down at the water below. "Your father—Mason—accused your uncle Will of making a pass at your mother."

"Uncle Will?" Becca whispered. "He never married, did he?"

Gram shook her head. "He was difficult, even as a child. Always set on his own rights, and he didn't care who he had to hurt to get what he wanted." Gram stopped and turned to look at Becca. "That's a terrible thing for a mother to have to admit."

Becca nodded. "What did Uncle Will say?"

Gram sighed and seemed to shrink even more. "It's not pleasant, Becca."

"Tell me. I can handle it."

"Can you?" Gram shook her head. "Very well. He told your father that you were his child."

His child. Something squeezed in her heart. She'd always noticed how different she looked from Jake and Wynne. Jake used to joke that she'd been left under a rock.

"I don't believe it," she whispered, but a part of her did.

Gram nodded. "I believed it at the time. Your parents had been arguing daily, and I'd caught Will and your mother in a rather compromising position in the garden. He was holding Suzanne. I couldn't tell if it was willing on her part or not."

"My mother would never be unfaithful!" Becca blurted. She felt horror at the thought she might not be who she thought she was.

Gram nodded. "I wish I didn't have to tell you this. I knew it would be upsetting." She tipped her head to one side and looked at Becca. "I have to say you look very much like Will, Becca. And if it's true, you would be Will's only heir. He was my oldest and it would be right and proper for you to inherit the house and grounds."

Becca flinched. "I don't want anything from you. Is there more?" She had to hear it all, though she wanted to bolt from the room.

"Things had been tense between Will and Mason. Your uncle Charles was very close to Mason so there was tension between Will and Charles, as well. Will goaded Mason and Charles tackled him. They fought ferociously at the top of the cliff. They both went over the edge. Charles—" Gram stopped and drew in a shaky breath. "Charles was killed and Will's body was never found."

"I would have thought you would have clung to my father even more," Becca whispered. She hated to sound as if she was accusing Gram, but she didn't understand.

Gram sighed then straightened her shoulders. "I blamed your mother. I told her I never wanted to see her again. Mason said that I'd never see him or you children, either, then."

Tears hung on her lashes when she stared in Becca's face. "I was foolish, so foolish. I forgot about you children, about my love for Mason, everything." She leaned heavily on the back of the chair.

"Surely Dad knew that. He wouldn't have accepted that." Becca's lips felt numb. Her perfect family wasn't so perfect after all.

"He tried to call me a few months later, but I was still grieving. I refused to take his call. He never tried again until two months ago when he called and said he was coming whether I wanted to see him or not. Of course I wanted him."

Becca thought her grandmother looked tired. "Maybe you should sit down," she said.

"I'm fine, Becca, just fine." Gram patted her hand. "It's just hard to admit I was so stupid."

"How did everyone else feel about Dad and Mom coming back?"

"Tate was upset. He thought he was only coming because he'd heard I had a heart attack and wanted to make sure he was in line to inherit."

"You had a heart attack?"

Gram nodded. "Just a mild one then, but the kids fretted. I'm fine, of course."

"That's what you always say," Becca said, smiling. She remembered that much about her grandmother. "Do you think Tate would have killed my parents?"

"Oh, goodness, no! Tate wouldn't hurt a flea. He's much too weak to run the risk of getting caught." Gram smiled wryly.

Becca wasn't so sure. She'd seen his anger with Shayna earlier in the day. And he seemed obsessed by money. "What about…Max?" She hated to even ask about her boss. She was beginning to like him more and more, even in the few days she'd been around him.

Gram paled. "He and Mason argued that last night."

Becca gulped. "What about?" This wasn't what she wanted to hear.

"My lawyer came that day, too, to begin drafting a new will." Gram looked at Becca piteously. "It did no good to tell them all I'd made those plans before your father called. It had nothing to do with their visit."

"What did they fight about?"

"Max wanted your father to understand Molly was to receive Laura's share, a share equal to that of you and your siblings together, not anything less."

"I'm sure Dad was fine with that."

"Actually, no, he wasn't. He thought the four of you should share equally. He didn't want anything for himself, but for the grandchildren to have what I left. The three of you and Tate. With Laura gone, he didn't think Molly had a share as a great-grandchild."

"This is terrible to be fighting over your property, Gram," Becca whispered. "I never would have thought my father would have any part of that."

Gram smiled sadly. "When it's your children involved, you do a lot of things that might surprise you. And it's a lot of money."

"What about Shayna? She likes to spend money."

Gram shook her head. "Shayna loves me. She's not as brittle as she appears at first. She's a lonely child looking for love and acceptance."

"I don't want your money, Gram," Becca burst out. "Give it all to Molly and Tate. Jake and Wynne won't care about it, either."

"Jake and Wynne. Where are they?" Gram's voice held a note of longing.

"Champing at the bit to see you, too. Jake is away on a dig, and Wynne is finishing up a marine project. They plan to come next month for sure."

"I want to see them," Gram said. She inhaled deeply. "I can't believe Max—or any of my family—would have any part in killing your parents."

"What about Bobby?"

Gram frowned. "Robert? You've been listening to

Max. He hates poor Robert, but the man is just trying to help his mother have a nest egg."

"What about Mrs. Jeffries? She gives me the creeps. She always has."

Gram laughed. "She's been with me forever, Becca. No, there's no one. I'm still not convinced they were murdered. Why do you think so?"

"I can't explain it, but I just know."

"Accidents happen, Becca. Terrible accidents," her grandmother said gently. "Sometimes we just have to accept those things as God's will."

"I *have* accepted it, but I don't want their murderer to go free!" Becca turned her back and went to stare out the window. The cold waters of Lake Superior were gray with an approaching storm. She turned back to face her grandmother.

"If it was an accident, why would someone want to kill me?"

Her grandmother gasped, and she went white. "What are you talking about?"

"Someone tried to roll a boulder on me the first week I was here."

"That's not possible." Her grandmother stood and grabbed both Becca's arms. "Tell me what you're saying."

Becca told her story, leaving nothing out.

"But why?" Her grandmother's bewilderment shone in her eyes. "No one knows who you are, right?"

"Someone must have figured it out," Becca said.

"Then you must leave. I can't lose you, too." Gram shook Becca gently. "Today."

"I'm not going anywhere. And you have to keep quiet about who I really am. Unless you want me to be in even more danger."

"No, of course not. But I want you to go, Becca."

For the first time, Becca saw a frail vulnerability in her grandmother's eyes. She hated that she had to worry her even more, but she had to say it…. "I'm staying."

Chapter Eight

W hy had Gram wanted to see Becca? Max stared at the closed door in frustration. He didn't trust the woman any more than he trusted Lake Superior in a rowboat. He wished he dared to join them, but he knew better than to upset Gram with her heart condition.

He stalked past the bedroom door and went down the steps to his office. Becca hadn't been much help with his research yet. He should have known better than to be taken in by her sweet talk on the phone, but the sound of her research paper had been intriguing. He was going to have to put his foot down tomorrow and insist she earn her wages.

This office was a mess. He stared at the jumble of books and papers with disfavor. Wasn't an assistant supposed to help organize things? It looked worse than before Becca had come. He gathered the books together in a pile and neatened up the desk.

His hand hovered over a computer printout. It looked like an e-mail, not research notes. Knowing he shouldn't pry but unable to stop the impulse, Max picked it up.

Becca, I wish you hadn't felt you needed to run off to the island—at least not until I could join you. I don't want anything to happen to you. Be careful. Love, Jake

So the lovely lady had a boyfriend. Max dropped the e-mail back onto the desk and told himself it was a good thing he knew about the man now. Becca was too tempting for his peace of mind. Now that he knew there was another man in the picture, it would be easier to keep his distance.

He jiggled his mouse to activate his computer screen. Staring at the blank screen, he wished he knew where to start this book. So far the beginning had eluded him. The stress of wondering what was happening in Gram's room upstairs didn't help his concentration.

"Daddy, I want to see Gram," Molly said from the doorway. "Her door is closed."

A smile tugged at his lips. Gram would never turn Molly away. He stood and joined his daughter. "Let's go roust her out," he said.

Gram had finally agreed to go along with Becca— if only to protect her. Seated beside her grandmother and sipping tea from Gram's favorite blue-and-yellow cups, Becca felt the last fifteen years had melted away.

A firm knock sounded on the door, and Max's voice echoed. "Gram? Molly is about to burst waiting to see you."

"Come in, my dear boy," Gram said. She put her cup and saucer on the table beside her chair. "I'm always ready to see my favorite girl."

Becca used to be her grandmother's "favorite girl." She pushed away the slight prick of jealousy. She was grown now, and she loved Molly, she reminded herself.

The door opened, and Molly burst into the room like a shaft of sunlight. She ran to Gram and climbed into her lap. "I missed you, Gram."

"I missed you, too, sweetheart." Gram wound a lock of Molly's hair around her index finger.

Becca sensed, rather than heard, Max enter the room behind his daughter. She could feel suspicion coming off him in waves. Her gaze traveled up to meet his, and she almost flinched at the distrust on his face. Had he heard their discussion? There were places in this old house where conversations could be easily overheard.

"Are you about ready to get back to work?" The question seemed mild enough, but Becca sensed a hidden rebuke in it.

"Sure." Becca jumped to her feet, nearly spilling her tea. "I'll talk to you later, uh—Mrs. Baxter."

"Call me Gram, please. Everyone else does."

Becca felt heat rise in her cheeks as Max raised an eyebrow. "Okay, Gr-Gram. I'll see you at dinner. Thanks for the tea." She put her empty cup on the table and went toward the door.

"If Molly gets too much for you, send her down to me," Max told Gram.

"Molly is never too much for me," Gram said stoutly. She adjusted the little girl on her lap and reached for a storybook on the bookshelf beside her chair.

Becca could feel the unspoken questions radiating from Max as they settled in at their respective desks. He drummed his fingers on the desktop, sighed, then typed a few words. He finally leaned back in his chair and swiveled around to look at her.

"What did Gram want?"

Becca bit her lip and kept her head buried in the thick book she'd been making notations on. "Um, nothing really. I think she just wanted to get to know me."

"That's not like her to call a private meeting." His suspicious gaze raked over her face.

She shrugged. "We just had tea, and I told her about visiting my grandmother in a place a lot like this one." Too late she realized that was the wrong thing to say. What place could be like this?

"I've never seen any place like Windigo Manor. Where did your grandmother live?"

"In Indiana," she said, thinking of her Grandma Phyllis's big Victorian house in Wabash.

"The cornfields of Indiana are nothing like Eagle Island," he said. "What did you talk to Gram about?"

Her head snapped and she stood. "Look, let's just get this out once and for all. What is it you're so suspicious of?"

"You're not who you seem," he said. "I think there's a lot you're hiding about who you are. I don't want the ones I love to be drawn into something that could hurt them. If someone really tried to kill you, then everyone here might be in danger, including my daughter."

"That's ludicrous!" she snapped. But was it? If the person who killed Becca's parents had done so for Gram's estate, then would Molly be next? Maybe she should tell Max her fears.

She rejected the idea as soon as it settled in her head. He might be the killer himself. If so, Molly was perfectly safe—it was Becca and Tate who might be in danger. But if Max wasn't the murderer, then Becca and Molly might be targets. She needed help from somewhere to watch out for all three of them.

She shook her head and shoved her pencil across the table. "Look, Max, I'm here to do a job. Will you please just let me do it? You're driving me crazy with your groundless suspicions. I'm no threat to you or your daughter or anyone else here."

"It sounds like you're saying you're a threat to someone though. What if he follows you here?"

"No one is following me here!" She stood and stalked to the window. She squinted at the distant boat on the waves of the lake. "I think someone might be in trouble out there!"

Max joined her at the window and grabbed the binoculars on the windowsill. "It's Shayna," he said. "I think her motor must have quit. I'd better get Tate and go after her."

"Do you need me to come?"

"No, you stay here. Work." He pointed at the books. "I'm sure she's fine." Calling for Tate, he bolted from the room.

After a few minutes, she heard the motorboat pull away from the dock. She diligently took notes for a while then got up to get a soda. Nick was in the kitchen poking through the refrigerator.

His face brightened when he saw her. "Want to scavenge with me? I'm starved."

"I just want a soda." She took the one he handed her and popped the top. "When do you have to go back to school?"

"Not until mid-August. You in a hurry to get rid of me?" He grinned as he took a bite of cheese.

"Of course not. I was just wondering. What do you do all summer?"

He shrugged. "Swim, body surf, lie in the sun."

"Sounds boring." She smiled to take the sting out of her words.

"Boring is good after dealing with thirty first graders all year."

"You teach first grade? How sweet."

"Don't say it like that. You make it sound like I'm some kind of wimp."

He was anything but a wimp. She glanced at his broad shoulders. "Sorry, I didn't mean anything by it. I think it's great you can teach kids. I'm not sure I'd have the patience."

"I'll make a good dad." He grinned. "Interested yet?"

She laughed. "Am I supposed to be?"

"I've been trying to get your attention ever since you walked in the door. So yeah, you're supposed to swoon at my feet."

"I'm not the swooning type."

"Rats. I knew I didn't have a chance. How about going to dinner with me tonight? I want to make it up to you for having to cancel on Friday."

"Where? Is there anywhere to go?"

"A greasy spoon in town. But at least we could get out for a bit."

"It's your grandmother's first night back."

"True. I notice you're not saying no though. How about next week?"

"Okay." She smiled. "It will be good to get away a bit. You are patient to persist."

He smiled. "Is Max driving you crazy yet? I would think working with him would take even more patience."

His tone sounded indulgent. "He can be a slave driver," she admitted.

Nick's smile faltered. "He's got a good heart though. Don't take offense and run off."

"It's sweet to see that you're close. I suppose that's why you're here this summer—to spend time with Max?"

Nick nodded. "Neither of us are overly close to our parents, but we've always been good friends. Max has always been there for me."

"He seems the type a person could lean on."

"He is, but don't be looking at him with an eye to romance. He's a woman-hater, in case you hadn't noticed. After Mom left, he's never trusted women."

"He was married."

"So? Lots of woman-haters get married."

Becca couldn't believe Max was really as he'd said. He seemed to relate to Gram and Molly just fine. It was herself he had issues with—and with good reason.

"Were he and Laura happy?"

"Did he actually mention Laura's name?" Nick's eyebrows went up. "Usually her name is never spoken."

Becca thought fast. "Um, no. I'm not sure where I heard the name. Maybe Molly."

"Molly misses her mother something fierce. Poor kid."

"What happened?" Becca tensed. The rumors she'd heard before she came whispered that Max might have been responsible.

"Boating accident. The engine exploded."

"Just like—" She bit off the final "my parents" before she gave herself away.

Nick looked at her curiously. "Like the Baxters? Yeah, I guess so. Strange things happen in these waters though. Superior is beautiful, but it's never safe."

"I thought she drowned."

"Well, she did. She was thrown from the boat by the explosion. Max, too. He tried to haul her to safety, but started getting hypothermia. He got so cold he couldn't feel his fingers. He lost his grip, and she went under and never came up again."

"Poor Max," she said with feeling.

He frowned. "I wouldn't have told you if I'd thought it would make him a romantic hero in your eyes. You just agreed to go out to dinner with me, and I want your attention. Leave my brother alone. He's not for you."

So in spite of their closeness, Nick had it in him to be jealous. Becca suppressed a smile. "I'm not getting any ideas about him. I'm not in the market for a relationship with anyone," she said.

"I take that as a personal challenge," Nick said, grinning.

She found herself smiling back. "Friends only," she warned.

"Fine. We can start there." He touched her cheek and went out the door.

Smiling and a little flattered, Becca went back to her desk. Men had never pursued her, and it felt strange for Nick to show his attraction so obviously. Strange but good.

She'd just finished notes on the Ojibwa culture book when she heard a commotion in the hall. Tate was shouting at Shayna, and Max was trying to calm him.

"How could you be so stupid?" Tate raged. "You didn't even check the gas."

"We aren't all obsessive-compulsives like you," Shayna retorted.

They'd seemed like the perfect couple when she'd first met them. Now all they did was squabble. Was it Max's fault? Tate seemed tense every time Max was around, and Becca knew he suspected his wife of having an affair with Max.

She was suddenly sick of this house and these people. She glanced at her watch. Five-fifteen, past quitting time. A breath of fresh air would help clear her thoughts. She grabbed her sweater and went out the office door so she didn't have to see or talk to anyone.

A stand of birch trees began where the garden ended, and she stepped into their cool shelter. She hadn't walked in these woods since she was a little girl. There was a tree around here somewhere with their names carved in it. Maybe she could find it.

The trees didn't seem as big as she remembered, but then neither did the house or the island. The scale of everything was different when she was five-ten instead of four-ten.

She saw the shed where she, Jake and Wynne used to play house. Gram had let them fix it up like a real playhouse. It was nearly falling down now. She would have thought Gram would have fixed it up for Molly, but maybe the little girl had never seen the possibilities as Becca and her siblings had done.

If she remembered correctly, the tree with their initials was just past the shed and to the right. Becca moved through the trees, last year's leaves crunching under her tennis shoes. A brisk breeze blew through her hair bringing with it the scent of wet leaves and wildflowers.

She remembered the crook in this tree. Her fingers ran over the rough bark, and she found the indentations. *RLB*. Rebecca Lynn Baxter. She still belonged here, even after so many years. Jake's initials were to the right of hers and Wynne's to the left.

Glancing up, she saw the tree platform where she and her siblings used to sit by the hour and watch. She'd often brought a book out here to read. Would it still be safe? Rounding the tree, she saw the rope ladder still attached. It looked as if someone had replaced some of the rungs, so maybe Molly still used it.

Or maybe not. Molly was a little young to be up a tree this size. Testing the strength of the rope, Becca put her right foot in a rung and began to climb. Halfway up, she made the mistake of looking down. The ground was a long way. If the ladder gave way beneath her now, she could easily break a leg.

She'd never worried about that as a child. Why was she so fearful now that she was an adult?

Turning from her downward stare, she began to climb again until she finally lay gasping on the platform in the tree's heart. From here, she could see almost straight into one of the bedrooms at the back of the house. She'd never noticed that before.

A figure passed in front of the window, and she realized it was Tate and Shayna's room. Shayna pushed back the curtains and sat at the desk in front of the window. Becca felt strange sitting here knowing she could see the other woman so clearly. She felt as though she was peeping.

She glanced around the platform. A pair of binoculars lay half-hidden by a sheaf of low-hanging leaves. Someone else liked to look through binoculars. Max.

Would he spend time up here looking through this pair? And if so, why?

Becca's gaze was drawn again to Shayna silhouetted in the window. She shivered. Had Max been watching Shayna? She remembered Tate's accusation about the affair. Was it more than that? Could Max be obsessed with Shayna and stalking her?

The brush rustled from the west. Someone was coming. Undecided about whether to stay hidden, she decided she'd better not be caught up here. She quickly clambered down and turned to face the tall form coming through the hedges.

Chapter Nine

Max looked out the window and saw a shadow flit from tree to tree in the white birch grove behind the house. He frowned. Occasionally a villager would come skulking onto the property to steal things. He'd better check it out.

He looked to make sure Molly was still occupied with Gram then went out the front door and slipped around the end of the house. A path led around the gazebo and entered the grove from the side. That would be his best entry point to catch the intruder red-handed.

The garden looked pristine and well manicured after the groundskeeper had pruned the shrubs. He walked along the row of evergreens shaped like barrels. The soft grass underfoot muffled his approach to the trees.

The shade welcomed him as he stepped into the trees. He heard muffled voices coming from the direction of the old milk house. Stepping softly, he trod in that direction. He parted the bushes and peered through. Becca stood talking with Nick.

Nick was standing too close to her for Max's liking.

She seemed not to mind though, as she tipped her head to listen to what his brother was saying. They made a nice couple, though she stood almost at eye level with Nick. He wanted to see his brother happy, but he had a feeling Nick needed some sweet little homebody who thought he hung the moon.

Becca was more likely to tell him to sit in his easy chair while she hung it herself. Max smiled at the thought.

She was nothing like Laura.

The unbidden thought made him frown. The last thing he wanted was to think about another woman in Laura's place.

He knew how the islanders whispered about him. The arguments they'd witnessed between Laura and him had fueled the speculation he'd had something to do with her death.

He pressed closer to hear what his brother was saying. Max was probably going to have to warn Becca off, and he didn't relish the thought of her fiery response. She didn't strike him as the type who would take kindly to someone meddling with her love life.

"Why are you asking so many questions about the boating accident?" Nick picked a flower and tucked it into Becca's hair.

She laughed, and her hand went to her hair. "I've just been hearing stories about it."

Was she talking about Laura's accident? She had no business poking her nose into his affairs. Max gritted his teeth. It was time he broke up this little tête-à-tête.

"There you are," he said, thrusting his leg through the brush.

Becca's face flushed, and Max wondered if it was because she felt self-conscious to be found with Nick or because she was afraid he'd overheard her prying into Laura's death.

He told himself he didn't care what Becca thought of him, but the assertion rang hollow.

"If you have something you want to know about my wife's death, ask me yourself, Becca. You don't need to go sneaking around asking questions behind my back."

Becca's startled gaze met his. "Your—your wife?"

"You idiot," Nick said. "We weren't talking about Laura. We were just discussing the boat that exploded a few weeks ago. Not everything revolves around you, you know."

Max's rage cooled into a puddle of embarrassment. "I heard you mention an accident, and I thought—" He broke off, well aware they knew what he thought. "Sorry," he muttered.

Nick turned to Becca. "My brother is paranoid. The villagers say he killed Laura."

Becca didn't gasp, though Max was sure she wanted to.

"I see," she said quietly.

Why did she always have to look at him with those eyes? Blue as Lake Superior and just as clear. Her eyes said there was no deceit in her soul, but Max knew better. There was some reason she was here on the island, and he intended to find out what it was.

"How did you hear about the boating accident?"

Becca looked away. "Molly's friend's mother mentioned it."

"I suppose she told you about everything that goes on around here, too, huh? I get sick of gossip. You'd do well not to listen to it."

"Why are you so defensive?" Her gaze met his again.

"I'm not. But I didn't hire you to indulge in gossip and pry into the affairs of this household."

"She wasn't prying. We were just talking," Nick protested.

"Oh, so you brought up the accident?"

His brother's gaze fell away, and Max knew Nick was just standing up for Becca. She had brought up the accident. What was her purpose? She was way too inquisitive, and he wanted to understand why. But looking at her set face, he knew it was a lost cause. At least today.

"I'll leave you two to your gossip." He turned and strode back through the brush. Let Nick look into her doe eyes and get sucked into her questions. She had an agenda, and Max was determined to discover what it might be. He had a private investigator friend in Houghton. He'd ask him to look into Becca's background.

Becca let out a shaky laugh. "I don't think Max likes me very much."

"Max doesn't like anyone much these days. Himself least of all."

"Why do you say that? Does he blame himself for his wife's death? He seemed defensive about that."

Nick nodded. "*Defensive*, that's a good word. He was navigating the boat, and when it exploded, he blamed himself for not having had it looked at. Laura had mentioned she smelled gas when she took it out a couple of days before the accident, and Max blew her off."

"The villagers think it was deliberate?"

"You know how people talk. He could have been killed as well. And Max may be gruff, but he's harmless."

"Did they get along? Is that what has fueled the gossip?" Becca felt terrible for prying into the man's private affairs, but if there was a connection to her parents' deaths, she had to find out.

"They had their squabbles. I think they'd been talking about divorce, but Max was trying to keep the marriage together for Molly's sake. He would have been devastated if Molly had left the island with her mother."

Upset enough to make sure that didn't happen? Becca bit back the words. She didn't really believe Max could be a murderer. Did she? She examined how she felt about the man and discovered she liked him more than she'd realized. She didn't want him to be guilty.

And a blind spot like that could get her killed.

"We'd better go inside," Nick said, his fingers touching her elbow. "The Windigo might be prowling tonight."

He said the words lightly, but a shiver still touched Becca's spine. The old superstitions were still lodged in her psyche. She allowed Nick to lead her through the brush toward the back of the manor.

She'd thought he might want to linger in the moonlight and steal a kiss or two and was relieved she didn't have to fend off a pass. Nick was an attractive man, but she found her thoughts straying to her boss more than she liked.

Nick left her in the hall. He needed to check in with Gram, he told her. Becca wandered down the hall to the library. Max was perusing a book with his back to her. She stood watching him a moment, then he turned and saw her.

"Done lingering in the moonlight with my brother?" His lip curled as he said the words, and Becca scowled at him.

"At least he's a gentleman, which is more than I can say about you."

"He's much too polite to be anything but gentlemanly. Whereas I on the other hand—" He broke off and in two strides was at her side. His fingers gripped her shoulders and he pulled her to him. His lips claimed hers, and Becca went rigid at first then softened as the harshness in the kiss changed to tenderness. Her fingers dug into his tweed sweater, and, feeling caught in a storm of emotion, she clung to him.

Her eyes were still closed when he released her.

"Sorry," he muttered.

She felt a shiver run through him, and his gaze was soft. He ran his fingers through his hair, leaving it sticking straight up.

"Maybe you'd better go find Nick again," he said. Still clutching his book, he turned and strode out of the room before Becca could muster enough coherent thought to answer him.

She touched her warm lips. What had brought that on? Could Max have been jealous of his brother? Until that kiss, she would have sworn Max didn't like her. She'd tried to tell herself she didn't find him attractive, but the kiss had shown that to be a lie. The sooner she discovered who had murdered her parents, the better. She needed to get out of here before her feelings for Max went beyond mere liking and attraction.

She'd have to be on her guard. She didn't want to get involved with a man who wasn't a Christian.

She heard a sound and turned to see her grandmother

sitting in the dark by the window. Her face burned at what she knew Gram had seen.

"Come here, Becca." Gram patted her lap.

"I'm too big to sit on your lap now," Becca said, going to her grandmother's side.

"You'll never be too big." Gram pulled her down onto her ample lap.

Becca felt like a giraffe perching on a child's stool. Her grandmother was maybe five-two while Becca towered at close to six feet tall. Still, the touch of Gram's hand on her hair brought back all kinds of great memories from her childhood. She nestled against her grandmother as best she could.

"Max is an attractive man," Gram said. "Tormented men always are."

"Are you warning me against him?"

"No, he's a good man, and he has a kind heart when someone bothers to look below the surface. But he's been through a lot. Don't hurt him, Becca."

"You're worried about me hurting him?" Becca sat up in astonishment. "I'm not the femme fatale type, Gram."

"You're lovely, Becca, you just haven't figured it out yet."

Lovely. No one had ever called her lovely. *Striking, Amazonian,* those were terms she'd heard before. *Lovely* had a nice feel to it. Warmth spread through Becca's chest.

"I don't think Max has anything to fear from me. You should be worried about me, not him. He could chew me up and spit me clear across the lake. Besides, I want a Christian."

"Of course you do. And Max would be a man worth

fighting for," Gram said. "He's close to coming to Christ. It would have happened before if not for Laura's death. Now he's finding it hard to trust, but he'll get it straightened out."

Becca blinked. "He seems totally self-sufficient."

"We used to have great discussions of God. I thought you'd read his books."

"I have."

"You've never noticed the struggle between good and evil in his stories? And good always wins."

Becca nodded. "I guess you're right." Could she help Max finally turn to God? She'd like to try. She glanced back at her grandmother. "Are you sure he didn't have anything to do with Laura's death?"

"Oh, my, no. Max is much too gentle for that. And he loved Laura, in spite of their problems. She was a willful child, always looking for excitement. I should have insisted they live on the mainland."

Gram's face grew pensive. "If the problems were anyone's fault, they were mine. Newlyweds shouldn't be living in a house with other people and catering to an old woman. I won't make that mistake again." Her faraway gaze cleared, and she smiled. "You'd better go to bed, Becca. You've had a busy day."

Becca was more than ready. She needed some time alone to assimilate the day.

She left her grandmother and went to her room. Moonlight filtered through the filmy curtains. Becca flipped on the light switch. Nothing. She toggled it again, but the light stayed off. Maybe the bulb was blown. She went across the room to the bedside table and clicked the switch on the bedside lamp. It didn't come on, either. Strange. The hall light was on so the house hadn't lost its power, a common occurrence on the island.

She started for the door to go get Max to see if he could figure out what had happened when she saw something on the bed. It looked like a doll. It was too dark to see clearly, so she picked it up. She carried it to the hall. The light illuminated the face of the doll, and Becca shuddered and dropped it.

A figure came up behind her, and she jumped. Mrs. Jeffries took hold of Becca's arm, and she winced at the housekeeper's strong grip.

"Where did you get that?" she demanded, looking down at the figurine on the floor.

"It was on my bed."

The woman's normally pale color seemed to bleach out even more. "There's evil afoot tonight," she muttered. She scooped the object up and stuffed it in her apron pocket.

"Wait, I wanted to show it to Max," Becca called after her retreating back, though nothing would induce her to touch the thing again.

It had looked to be made out of twigs, and the leering grin on its face had made her heart skip. The teeth in the thing's mouth were pointed and nasty looking. Mrs. Jeffries had used the word *evil,* and Becca thought it an appropriate word for how the doll made her feel.

She told herself not to be silly. God was her protector, and there was no power in a fetish like the figurine. All the same, she was glad she didn't have to look at it any longer.

"What's the commotion?" Max came out of his room. Still dressed in his jeans and shirt with tweed sweater, he looked calm.

His solid presence made Becca feel safe, and her stomach began to settle. "Someone left a nasty present on my bed," she told him.

He raised his eyebrows. "Oh?"

"Some kind of fetish. It looked like it was supposed to be a Windigo figurine." She shivered. "The legends say the Windigo has huge teeth, and this thing's teeth took up half the head."

He frowned. "Are you okay?"

Becca forced a smile. She refused to show her fear. "Oh, sure. But could you look at my lighting? None of the lights are working." He followed her to her room and checked it.

"The lightbulbs are tight," he said. "Let me check the breaker box."

Becca followed him downstairs to the utility room. He swung open the breaker box cover.

"We used to get power outages all the time, but this is the first problem since we put in the new breaker box." He inspected the labeled breakers. "The one to your room is flipped off," he said. His frown deepened. "That's strange. I wonder who's been in here. We haven't had any electrical work done that I know of. I'll ask Moxie about it."

Becca felt cold suddenly. It had to have been someone in the house. But why? No one knew who she was.

She followed Max out of the utility room and stood by the door while he questioned Mrs. Jeffries in the kitchen. Mrs. Jeffries stood stiffly and gestured with clenched hands as Max questioned her. They spoke in low voices, and Becca couldn't hear all that was said, but it was obvious from the woman's stance that she resented Max's line of questioning.

Max rejoined her. "She says it's a warning for you to leave the house."

"You don't think she put it there, do you?" Mrs. Jeffries had seemed truly upset when she found the figurine, but some people found it easy to hide the truth.

"Why? What could she have against you? For that matter, I don't understand why anyone would try to warn you away. You've only been here a week. That seems hardly long enough to make enemies." His gaze lingered on her face. "Don't you think it's time you told me why you're really here?"

Becca took a step back and looked away from his penetrating eyes. Those eyes looked as if they could read every secret in her soul as easily as he read his computer. "I don't know what you mean," she stammered.

"I think you do. I didn't have an ad out for an assistant. You called me out of the blue. Why would you want to come here? Your explanation didn't ring true then, and it sure doesn't now, either. I think there's a reason you're hiding out here. A man? Someone after you?"

Relief flooded Becca. "I'm not hiding out from some man. I told you when I called that a friend had told me you could use an assistant."

"That's lame, Becca. Really lame. I'm not sure why I didn't question it more when you fed me that line. But I'm questioning it now. What friend? I want to know the truth."

What did she tell him? Becca thought frantically. She couldn't lie. Not telling her real last name was bad enough. She took a deep breath and blurted out the first thing that came to mind. "I used to come here for the

summers. I'd always admired this old house. I wondered what it would be like to get a chance to live here."

Had his face softened just a fraction? She studied the
rigid line of his jaw. Maybe not. He still looked mad
enough to spit.

"I used to play with Laura," she said.

His mouth sagged. "What? You knew Laura?"

Too late she realized it was the wrong thing to say.

"So you *are* investigating her death, prying and dig-
ging into things you have no business sticking your
nose in."

"No, no, I'm not interested in Laura's death. I—I
didn't mean that," she stammered.

"I want you to pack up your things and leave on the
ferry tomorrow," he said firmly.

"No!" Molly hurtled into the room and threw herself onto Becca's legs. "I like her, Daddy. You can't
send her away."

Becca knelt beside Molly. "Don't worry, Molly. I'm
not going anywhere." She sighed. "You'd better get to
bed. I need to talk to your daddy."

Chapter Ten

Max stood with his arms folded across his chest. He was surprised to find a keen sense of disappointment in Becca residing in his heart. Though he'd been suspicious of her, the knowledge that she'd played him for a patsy rankled more than he'd thought it would. There had been something different about the young woman, something that tugged at his emotions in ways he hadn't felt in a long time.

"Well?" he asked when she shut the door behind Molly. "This had better be good."

She wet her lips, and he saw the fear in her eyes. She was afraid of him? The startling thought made him drop his gaze and look away.

"I'm not here to pry into Laura's death," she said quietly.

"Then why are you here? And don't tell me it's for the job. I'm not that stupid."

"I—I knew the people who died on the boat last month. I was trying to find out about the explosion."

"How did you know them?"

She looked away. "I'd rather not say."

"I think you'd better."

She hadn't been looking at him as she spoke, but she looked up from her studied perusal of the carpet at his sharp tone. Her chin jutted out. "No. Gram knows and that's all that matters. That's all I'm saying. But I'll continue to do the best job I can with your work. You need me, Max, and you know it."

He scowled. She was right about that. He needed someone to organize his notes and help keep him on track. It was unlikely he could find someone else to come out here. And Molly loved her. But was she more trouble than she was worth? He was beginning to think so.

He sighed and chewed on his lower lip. It could wait until he had her investigated. Maybe he'd be far enough along in his work to be able to do without her then.

"You can stay," he said abruptly. "But stay out of family business. It doesn't concern you."

She didn't respond to his terse comment but merely nodded and turned to leave. She turned back around. "I can see under that gruff exterior, Max. You're not as tough as you'd like people to believe. And God still loves you, even if you don't believe it."

Her tall, willowy figure slipped out the door. Max closed it behind her. What did she know about the way God had deserted him? He glanced at his watch. Nearly nine o'clock. Adam should still be up. He grabbed the phone and dialed the number.

"Hey, Adam," Max said when his old college friend answered the phone. "I've got a rush job for you. Find out what you can about a Becca Lynn." He told Adam what he knew and gave him Becca's last address. His friend promised to see what he could find out.

Max hung up the phone and went to the window. The moonlight glimmered on Lake Superior's waves. To the west, he could see the Rock Harbor lighthouse on the mainland flicker on and off. The old lighthouse had been dark for years until Bree Nicholls had restored it. Now the beacon guided ships through dangerous waters, and Max often wished there was a beacon like that for him. He felt adrift these days, rudderless.

Becca's arrival had sparked a yearning he'd had when talking to Gram in the old days. Gram would say it was God tugging at him, and maybe that's what was happening. He didn't know if that was a good thing or bad.

Becca's pulse still throbbed as she escaped to her room. Max wouldn't let things ride for long. She could sense his impatience to know the truth. He'd get it out of her before too long. It was all she could do not to spill all of it when his gaze pinned her to the wall. She had to maintain her composure long enough to discover the truth. Max was still a suspect himself. They all were. She had to remember that.

Her room felt tainted as her eyes fell on the bed where the figurine had been. A trickle as cold as Superior ran up her spine. She fell to her knees beside the bed and prayed for safety and for God to cleanse this room of the evil that had been here.

"Help me to be a light in the darkness here, Lord," she whispered as she got up and wiped her eyes. She had to lean on God for courage because right now she wanted to turn and run.

This place needed light. Through the window she could see the lighthouse beacon flash on and off. She hadn't done a very good job the last few days. Sometimes the darkness seemed overwhelming. The lighthouse never tired of its job out on the water, and she needed to have that same steadfastness.

Her grandmother would be a haven for her. She glanced at her watch. Would Gram still be up? One way to find out. She slipped out the door and tiptoed down the hall. A light shone from under Gram's bedroom door. Becca tapped lightly on the door.

"Come in." Gram's voice sounded strong and alert.

Becca heard a sound down the hall to the left. She stepped quickly into Gram's bedroom and shut the door behind her. Her heart hammered against her ribs, and she prayed no one had seen her enter her grandmother's room. It would be sure to arouse suspicion for the secretary to be spending time with the house owner for no apparent reason. She was going to have to watch how she interacted with Gram.

Her grandmother was propped in bed on three pillows with her Bible in her hand. Her face brightened when she saw Becca.

"I was just praying for you, my dear," she said, holding out her hand. "You look upset. What is it?"

"Max is suspicious of me," Becca said, hurrying to the bed. "He was ready to throw me off the island."

"We can't have that," Gram said.

Becca could see the wheels turning in Gram's head. "I have an idea," her grandmother said. "The kids have been after me to do something about my books. Do you have any bookkeeping experience?"

"Yes, I have a minor in business," Becca admitted. Of course, she also had minors in art history, interior design and economics, though she didn't admit it. She didn't want her grandmother to know she'd been such a flake in college and had changed her major so many times she'd spent six years in school.

"Perfect. I'll tell Max he has to share you, and that I want you to keep my books and help me get organized. What are your hours with him?"

"Nine to three."

"We'll change those to nine to one and you can work on my books for a couple of hours a day."

"He'll be angry," Becca warned.

"Most likely. But there will be nothing he can do about it. And he can't send you packing without my permission," her grandmother said with obvious satisfaction. "I can take his bellowing."

"I'm not sure I can." Becca shuddered. "He was so angry with me tonight."

"His bark is worse than his bite." Gram pulled her down and kissed her quickly on the cheek. "Now get out of here before someone finds you. Look into the hall before you go out." Her cheeks were flushed as though she was enjoying the secrecy.

Becca suppressed a smile. This was likely the most excitement her grandmother had experienced in years. She kissed her grandmother's soft cheek then went to the door. She put her ear against it and listened. Nothing. Turning the knob silently, she poked her head out of the door and looked. The hall looked empty. She slipped through the door and closed it behind her as quietly as she could.

She sped down the hall toward her door, nearly reaching it before she saw a dark figure at the top of the stairs.

"I just knocked on your door." Tate stepped out of the shadows. "What were you doing in Gram's room?"

He'd seen her. Becca's heart sank, and she fumbled for an answer. "Um, she has some work she wants me to do for her."

Her cousin's eyes widened. "What work could Gram have to do?"

"Accounting stuff, I guess. She wants me to help organize her books a couple of hours a day."

"I wonder what brought that on," Tate said thoughtfully. "We've all been after her for years to do something about her affairs. Max has been in charge of her buying supplies and keeping an eye on her finances, but that's been as far as it's gone."

"It shouldn't take long to get her books in order," Becca said.

"She probably thought now would be the time with a secretary in the house." Tate smiled.

"Why were you looking for me?" Becca asked.

"I wanted to thank you."

"For what?"

"Shayna has been lonely for female companionship. She really likes you, and it was good of you to befriend her."

Becca's heart warmed toward her cousin. In spite of his problem with alcohol, he must love his wife. "I like Shayna. I didn't do it as a favor. I need a friend as well."

Tate smiled, but there was sadness in his eyes. "I haven't been the best husband."

He stared at Becca, and she saw a hint of desperation in his gaze. "Is there anything I can do?" she asked him.

"You're a praying woman," he said. "You might think to ask God to help me get this demon off my back."

"You could ask him yourself."

Tate shook his head. "I used to go to church all the time, and God and I were on a first-name basis. Then, little by little, I got caught up in other things. Now look at me." He smiled wryly. "God has probably forgotten all about me."

"I know that's not true," Becca said softly. "God still loves you, Tate. He has never stopped."

Tate smiled. "You'd make a good preacher, Becca."

She could see he wasn't going to talk about it anymore. "I'll pray for you, Tate."

"You know, you remind me of someone. I've been trying to put my finger on it ever since you came, but I can't seem to remember. Another benefit of drinking." He lifted his beer in a silent toast. "It will come to me."

As he walked away, Becca could only pray he never remembered. They'd been close as children. She was surprised it had taken him this long to realize she was familiar. She hoped the memories would elude him until she was free to reveal who she really was. She resolved to pray he'd turn his life around.

The next morning Becca approached the dining room with trepidation. She'd barely slept last night as she wondered what Max would say when Gram revealed her plan to him. A heavy cloud cover with accompanying drizzle dampened her mood even more.

The weather seemed to have affected everyone in the house. Becca stepped into the dining room and went to her place. Her grandmother greeted her with a smile, but the rest of the group barely grunted at her good-morning. Even Molly seemed subdued.

Mrs. Jeffries brought in the platters of eggs and pancakes, and everyone passed the food with little discussion.

Shayna glanced at Becca. "I suppose you want to pray."

At least it was getting easier. Sometimes courage worked like that. Start down a path and it got easier.

Becca exchanged a glance with Gram.

Gram cleared her throat. "You've all been after me to get my affairs in order, so I've decided to do just that. Becca here has graciously agreed to help me out. Max, I'd like her at one every day for a bit. Once I get organized, a few hours a week will likely suffice."

Max gaped, and Becca suppressed a grin. "I need her myself, Gram," he said finally. "Once I have my notes more fully in order, it would be easier."

"I realize it may put you back a few weeks, but I'll pay her salary for you so that won't be an issue."

Becca had never seen this inflexible side of her grandmother. From Gram's tone, it was clear Max had no choice.

Max didn't seem to take the hint. "It's still an issue. I'd like to help, but Becca is *my* employee, not yours. I'll pay her salary, and she'll answer to me, not you. I can spare her a few hours a week, but that's all. If Becca agrees to work for you, she'll need to do it after the hours I need her. She's done at three. She could work until five for you." He glanced at Becca as if daring her to contradict him.

"Those hours are too long," Gram objected. "How about if we compromise, and Becca joins me from two to three? It will take a bit longer to get my office organized, but it can still be done."

Max frowned then shrugged. "Okay, I guess I can live with that."

"Let's not fight this morning," Tate said in a weary voice.

Tate's face was pale, and Becca wondered if he had a hangover or if he'd just gotten up on the wrong side of the bed.

"That's all settled," Gram said. "I'd like to get started today."

Becca smiled at Gram's wink. "Okay by me. Thanks, Gram."

"Then we'd better get to work." Max shoveled one last bite of pancake into his mouth and stood.

"Max, really! Poor Becca hasn't had a bite to eat yet," Shayna chided.

She had taken to visiting with Becca every evening and they discussed the books they'd been reading. Becca warmed at Shayna's defense of her, and gave her a grateful smile.

Shayna smiled back. "Sit down and enjoy your breakfast. The world won't end if your story takes two weeks longer than you'd hoped."

Max didn't answer Shayna, but went toward the door. "Finish your breakfast, Becca. I'll see you in my office when you're done."

"That man," Shayna said when Max had left the room. "He is so driven."

"He has good reason to be," Gram said gently. "He's feeling he can't write anymore, and a comment like you just made makes him feel what he does is unimportant. You really should apologize, Shayna."

"He knows I don't feel that way," Shayna said. "I'm one of his biggest fans."

"I love his writing, too," Becca said. "I've read everything he's ever written. His characterization is phenomenal. I'd read his laundry list."

Too late she realized she sounded like a groupie. She smiled feebly. "He really is remarkable. I'm glad for the opportunity to work with him."

Gram's smile was warm and approving. "You might try telling him that, Becca."

Becca nodded and picked at her food. The bickering had dispelled any hunger she'd had. She finally pushed her plate away and got up. "I'd better get to work."

"I'll see you at two," Gram called after her.

Becca nodded and went to Max's office. The few bites of food she'd managed lay in her stomach in a hard knot.

Max was bent over his computer. He straightened up when she entered the room. "I want to know one thing," he said.

"What's that?" Becca went to her desk and pulled a book toward her.

"How did you get Gram to agree to letting you help her?"

"It was her idea."

"I find that hard to believe." He stared at her steadily until she looked away.

"It's the truth," she said. "I didn't even know she needed any help, so how could it have been my idea?"

"I want to know how you know Mason and Suzanne Baxter," Max muttered. "I don't like all this secrecy."

Becca sighed. "Let's just get to work."

He shoved a stack of papers away. "I'm warning you—don't do anything to hurt Gram. I love her, and you won't like the consequences if I ever find out you've stepped over the line."

"I love her, too," Becca protested.

"You don't know her that well. Or so you claim." His eyes narrowed, and his nostrils flared.

Caught. She looked away. "She's a darling. Anyone can see that," she said.

"Yes, she is. She's always been there for me, and I will always be here for her. So take that as a warning."

"You don't have to worry about me," Becca said.

"Oh, I am. But I'm watching you, as well. You're going to have to tell me the rest of it sooner or later. I'd rather it be sooner, but I can wait. I'm good at waiting."

Becca knew how a mouse felt when it was trapped in a hole by a patient cat. Maybe her brother and sister could come soon. She could use an ally. The heavy load of what she had to accomplish nearly crushed her shoulders. But she'd do this. Her parents deserved that much.

She looked at the desk. "What do you want me to do first?"

"Just keep working on taking notes of pertinent Ojibwa legends. Group them by type of legend."

She nodded and got to work. When she ran across the section on the Windigo, she sat up and paid even closer attention. According to the three books she had looked at, some researchers thought the legends may have started with men who contracted rabies or who went insane from the isolation of the far north.

That didn't apply here. Becca's thoughts wandered to the figurine left on her bed last night. Mrs. Jeffries seemed the most likely culprit, in spite of her professed horror at seeing it. She was the one who talked about the Windigo all the time. What if she had recognized Becca and wanted her gone? But that still didn't answer the question of why. Becca was no threat to the housekeeper.

Becca sighed and pushed the book away. Her head ached from the sleepless night and the stress of the last few days. She longed to kick off her shoes and wander in the sand, though looking at the inclement weather, that wasn't a good option today.

Max leaned back in his chair and rubbed his eyes. "It's nearly lunchtime. Molly is supposed to go to her friend's for a sleepover. Would you care to ride along? There's an Ojibwa burial site I thought we might stop and see on the way home."

"Today?" Becca glanced at the wet, gray skies.

"You afraid you'll melt?"

His derisive tone smarted and implied he knew she wasn't sugar. "Not at all," she said. "I'm game. I was wanting a break anyway."

"Bring an umbrella and stout shoes. It's not an easy walk."

Even as she nodded and went to gather her things, Becca wondered if it was safe to go off with Max. Accidents happened, and he wouldn't be held accountable for it.

Chapter Eleven

Molly chattered the entire way to town. Max tried to answer her questions, but his attention kept wandering to the woman beside him. Becca hadn't wasted any time in gaining an ally in Gram. How had she done it? There hadn't been time last night, and he'd been up early this morning. There were so many undercurrents in this situation, he felt he was swimming against a whirlpool in Lake Superior.

He pulled up in front of the Anderson home. Molly hopped out, and he promised to pick her up in the morning. Saija waved from the doorway. Becca waved back with what seemed to Max to be extreme vigor. They'd certainly become close in the one short visit.

Becca seemed to have a way of getting to people. Even Max had to admit he found her appealing. She was more than lovely to look at, and she had a dogged persistence he admired. Whatever had brought her here, she wasn't a quitter.

"Ready for lunch?" he asked.

She nodded. "I'm famished."

They ate in a smoky room at Bob's Eats, and Becca kept remarking on how delicious the pasties were. Max had forgotten the way people who didn't live in the Upper Peninsula found pasties so unique. It was such a staple up here, a rich mixture of beef, rutabaga, potatoes, and onions combined into a savory pie with a thick folded crust.

"So tell me where you grew up," Max said. He tried to keep his tone light and conversational.

Becca shot him a glance that told him she knew exactly what he was up to. She bit into her pasty and took her time about chewing.

"I grew up in Chicago," he said. "This is a world apart from there." Maybe if he offered some background of his own, she'd be more forthcoming.

"I love shopping in Chicago," she said. "The stores along Michigan Avenue seem endless."

"Laura always liked it, too." He shouldn't have said anything about Laura. Becca already thought he killed his wife. At least that was the only reason he could find for the suspicion he often found in her eyes.

"How did you meet your wife?"

"I was teaching history at the University of Chicago, and she was my assistant."

Becca nodded. "She was quite lovely." She colored and dropped her gaze. "From her pictures, I mean. I only knew her as a child, but even then she attracted a lot of attention."

Max narrowed his gaze, and stared at her. He wanted to know more about the time she'd spent on the island, but he knew better than to ask. She would just clam up. This whole thing had him so perplexed, he didn't know which way was up. "Yes, she was."

"I was raised in Wyoming," she said. "Which seems strange to me now. I haven't been there in nearly five years."

At last she was opening up. "Where did you go to school?"

"Indiana University."

"What was your major?"

"English Literature." She didn't meet his gaze, and he wondered if she was lying about that. It would be one place for Adam to start looking.

"Do you still keep in touch with friends there?" he probed.

She nodded. "My roommate and I got an apartment together when we graduated. She was from Chicago, too."

"Was she upset when you took off to the great north country?"

"It was good timing. She was about to go off to Europe with her parents for the summer."

"What's her name?" He tried not to show his excitement.

Becca looked away and pointed out the window. "There's Tate. Wonder what he's doing here?"

Max turned to look and saw Tate talking to an older man dressed all in denim and wearing a Tigers hat. "That's Bob Chester, the boat builder. Tate has been saying he wanted to buy a new sailboat. Guess he was serious."

"I was under the impression Tate and Shayna had some money problems," Becca said.

Max looked at her sharply. "You don't miss much," he said.

"I overheard them arguing about money."

"I think they do okay, but Tate thinks she spends too much."

"Does she?" She twisted her dolphin necklace around her index finger.

"Don't most women?"

"You sound a little bitter. Was Laura a spendthrift?"

He was supposed to be questioning her, but she somehow always managed to turn things around. Max stood. "We'd better get out to the Ojibwa burial ground."

Becca dropped her napkin on her plate and stood. "Whatever you say."

"I'll remind you of that later," he said with a grin. Even though he didn't trust her, he liked her. He wished he didn't.

Her long stride kept up with his. "What are you hoping to find at the burial grounds?"

"Names, anything that might jog an idea for this book. It's amazing what you find in a cemetery."

They drove along a dirt track with encroaching bushes brushing the truck at each side. Becca was clinging to the armrest with grim determination on her face as the truck bottomed out on several of the pits in the road. Though the rain had stopped, the moisture had turned the road into a muddy quagmire.

"Sorry," Max said. "It's the only way out here."

"I'm fine," she said. "It's beautiful out here."

Max hadn't noticed, but now that she'd said something, he saw the lush greenery and timberline with new eyes. "No one comes out here much anymore." He pulled into a nearly hidden lane and stopped the truck. "We have to walk from here. It's about ten minutes."

The sound of the waves was muffled by the trees. At

last, saying, "The lake is just over the cliff here," Max held the brush for her, and they stepped into the clearing. Broken headstones amid thick grass dotted the clearing at the top of the cliff. Beyond it rolled the whitecaps of Lake Superior, louder now without the trees.

"What a charming spot." Becca approached the closest headstone and knelt down to look. "Rose Running Horse. Died 1875 when shot by a hunter."

"See what I mean," Max said, scribbling down the notation. "There's a story in those simple words. What was the hunter doing? Was it accidental or murder? Was she where she shouldn't have been?"

"I'll never understand the creative process," she said. "I don't know if I've ever told you, but I think you have the most amazing voice in fiction today. I'd read your laundry list if there was nothing else coming."

A flush of pleasure heated his veins. "Is that why you contacted me?" When she looked away, he felt cold. This was just another ploy to breach his defenses. She was calculating and knew how much her words would affect him.

"Over here," he said curtly. He stalked to another row of tombstones. "Write down anything interesting you see. I'll check the next row over." The sooner he figured out what she wanted from him and got her off the island, the better.

Becca's hand ached from writing. Max had turned all prickly when she'd told him how much she liked his writing. She knew her silence when he'd asked her if that was why she'd called for the job had bothered him. He probably thought she hadn't meant it. She hated these half-truths. A Christian was supposed to be honest, and she'd been anything but forthcoming. She'd comforted herself with the knowledge that she hadn't exactly *lied,* but the assertion was failing to bring her relief from her guilt.

She needed a break. Max was clear over at the other end of the clearing, and she was too tired to go tell him. He'd never miss her for a few minutes. She saw a path lined with rock that led along the cliff face to a set of steps carved out of the rock. The sun was hot now that the storm had blown past, and the glistening sand beckoned.

She put her pad and paper down on a flat rock and walked along the top of the cliff. There was a rope to hang on to as she went down the rocky steps, but it looked rotten and frayed, so she didn't dare put too much faith in it.

As she neared the bottom of the steps, she began to hear a tuneless whistle. Curious, she wandered in the direction of the sound.

A man stood stretching his fishing nets over the rocks. His muscular back was clad in a faded blue shirt, and she couldn't see his face. His curly black hair glistened with perspiration.

She thought to back away and continue on her way undetected, but the man turned and saw her. His features came into focus, and a vague sense of familiarity nudged her.

"Hello," he said, shading his eyes with his hand.

"Hi," she said, trying to place him.

"You visiting here?" he said. He dropped his net and came closer. "I'm Greg Chambers."

No wonder he looked familiar. He was Saija's

cousin. Becca's gaze traced the line of strong jaw and firm lips. He'd been cute as a seventeen-year-old boy. He was handsome and virile as a thirty-eight-year-old man. She'd spent her last summer here mooning over him. He'd helped the gardener one summer and had been at the house nearly every day, though he'd paid more attention to Laura than to her.

"Yes, at the Baxters' house," she said.

He stopped then and his gaze probed her face. "Becky. Saija told me you'd come back."

Heat rushed to her face. "Hello, Greg."

"You weren't going to tell me who you were," he stated. "I'm sorry about your parents."

"You can't tell anyone you saw me," she said.

He frowned. "What's going on?"

"I'm trying to find out what happened to my parents, and I don't want anyone to know who I am," she said. "So please don't give me away."

He looked past her, and his genial expression changed, and she saw anger and hatred vie for control of his face. "Here comes your murderer," he hissed. He stepped back and began to spread his net with jerky movements.

Becca turned and saw Max coming toward her across the sand. He wore a scowl identical to Greg's.

"I wondered where you'd gone," he said. "I'm ready to go if you can tear yourself away from the young Adonis here."

The contempt in his voice rattled Becca. "I—I'm ready," she stammered.

"You got something to say, say it to my face," Greg spat, turning to face Max.

"You're not worth my time." Max's lip curled.

"Hotshot writer, you think you know it all." Greg's face grew crimson. "You didn't know enough to keep your wife happy, did you?"

Max's hands curled into fists. "We were perfectly happy until you interfered."

Becca was beginning to get it now. Greg must have been the other man she'd heard about.

"You just couldn't stand for her to be happy, could you?" Greg stepped closer and thrust his face into Max's. "You won't get away with it. Someday people will know you killed her."

Greg's face crumpled, and Becca thought he was going to cry. She could see his hands shake.

"I didn't kill my wife," Max said quietly.

Greg's face flushed even more. "She and I were going to move to Marquette and start a new life. You couldn't stand that, could you?"

"You're delusional, Chambers. You weren't the first man in Laura's life. She liked the excitement of the chase. Once she caught a man, she grew bored with him. It was just a matter of time before she dumped you. I'm sorry for you, I really am." He turned and grabbed Becca's arm. "Let's go."

"You're wrong!" Greg shouted after them. "You'll pay, Duncan. I'll make sure you pay."

Becca could barely keep up with Max. His angry strides carried him past the steps, and she tugged at his arm and pointed. "We go up here."

He turned and helped her mount the first step. "You go first." His voice was terse and angry.

Becca dared a peek at him. A muscle in his jaw worked, and she could sense a coiled strength in him. "I'm sorry," she said.

"Stay away from Chambers," he said. "He's bad news. I'm not convinced he didn't have something to do with Laura's death. He was the last person to work on the motor."

"Could he have wanted to kill you and not Laura?" Becca was breathless as she struggled up the steep steps.

"Laura seldom went out in the boat with me."

"Why did she go that morning?"

Max reached the top of the cliff where Becca stood. "I've never figured that out. I was going fishing, and she hated the smell of fish. She said she wanted to talk to me." He shrugged. "Maybe Chambers was right, and she was really leaving me. She might have wanted to get me alone where no one could hear us yell at one another."

Becca felt rattled as she walked back to the car with Max. She wasn't finding out much about her own parents, but Laura's death was steeped in mystery, as well.

Max fairly vibrated with anger as he drove back to the house. It always upset him to see Chambers. And even though he didn't want to admit it to himself, he'd been overcome with jealousy to see Becca talking to the man. She deserved someone with more integrity than one who was willing to get involved with a married woman.

He reined in his thoughts. Where had that come from? Becca was a deceiver of some kind and she deserved whatever she got. He needed to keep his distance. He glanced at her from the corner of his eye and realized that was easier said than done.

He parked the truck in front of the manor and jumped out. Becca followed him inside.

She put her hand on his arm as they reached the porch. "I'm sorry, Max," she said. "I hate that Laura hurt you, and that you're still in pain over it."

Looking down into her earnest blue eyes, Max believed her. Whatever she might be hiding, her compassion and gentleness were evident. "Thanks," he said. The tension began to ebb from his tight muscles. His hand covered hers, and she blushed but didn't remove it.

"I know you're suspicious of me, Max," she whispered. "But I'm no threat to you."

"I'm not so sure about that," he said in a low voice. "I think you're dangerous to my peace of mind, Becca Lynn." She was so close now he could feel her breath on his face. He gave up the struggle and bent his head to kiss her.

Her lips were warm and welcoming, then he could feel her withdrawal before she actually pulled away.

"We shouldn't do this," she said.

"Why not? I'm not taken and neither are you. Are you?"

"N-no," she stammered. "But I don't want you to repeat a past mistake. I'm your assistant, just like Laura was. It might be another case of being in close proximity."

She might have a point. He dropped his hand from her arm. "You'd better go inside," he said.

She gave him one last look then rushed inside. He could have sworn he saw tears on her lashes, and he hoped they weren't his fault. He waited a few minutes then went inside.

"You had a phone call while you were gone," Shayna said. "Your friend, Adam."

Max was wishing he hadn't asked Adam to check out Becca. She might be hiding something, but he wanted to believe it was nothing that concerned him. He nodded to Shayna then went to his office to call Adam.

"What's up, buddy?" he asked.

"You sure you gave me the right name?" Adam asked.

"I'm sure. Why, what did you find?"

"There's no record of a Becca Lynn at Indiana University. And the address you gave me belongs to Sherri Lambdon."

Max hung up the phone. Everything Becca had said was a lie. So much for believing her lies. He wanted to toss her out on her ear, but Gram would have a fit. It would take more subtlety than simply confronting her like a raging bull.

He glanced toward the stairs. She would be working with Gram this afternoon, and her room would be empty. Maybe he could discover some clue to her true identity—and even more importantly—to what she was doing here on Eagle Island.

He waited until he saw Becca go off with Gram then went to the bedroom. In two minutes, he'd found her purse. Her picture on her driver's license was dark but easily identifiable as Becca. The name on it didn't sink in at first. Rebecca Lynn Baxter. *Laura's cousin.*

No wonder she'd offered to help Gram. She was here to make sure she was Gram's heir. Max gritted his teeth. She couldn't be allowed to take away what belonged to Molly.

Chapter Twelve

Gram was waiting for Becca when she got home with Max. Her blue eyes were as bright as polished turquoise, and she quivered with excitement as she showed Becca the mishmash of papers and receipts in her desk.

"I know I should have done something about this long ago," she said. "It will be fun now with you here. You can tell me things I missed while you were growing up—like your first boyfriend, learning to drive, your relationship with Jake and Wynne. I long to see them, too."

"They're planning on coming to the island in a few more days," Becca said. She needed allies and longed to see her siblings. "I hope to find out more about the boat explosion before they come. It will be difficult to keep their identity secret."

"We'll think of something." The glow in her grandmother's eyes dimmed. "I still think you're wrong, Becca. The explosion had to be a terrible accident, not murder."

"Then why is someone trying to get rid of me?"

Becca shook her head. "It's the only explanation, Gram."

"I can't bear to think that any of my family would deliberately cause harm," Gram said, dropping into the chair by the window.

"Tell me more about all of them," Becca prompted as she began to organize the receipts into piles of categories.

"Well, let me see. Let's start with Tate." Her smile dimmed further. "I love that boy, but I could shake him. He's let the demon of alcohol control his life."

"He talked to me about it. I think he sees it and would like to change. We talked about God."

Gram's head came up at that, and she beamed at Becca. "I knew you'd be good for this family, my dear. Keep up your testimony with him."

"I'm not sure what kind of testimony I'm having. I'm not being honest with anyone, and it's grating on me."

"I wondered if the Holy Spirit would let you get by with half-truths."

"You think I should reveal who I am?"

"God always honors truth. I know you feel the danger will be more if your identity is known, but sometimes you just have to do what's right and trust God with the outcome."

Heat flooded Becca's cheeks. "I'm being a coward, aren't I?" It was just like being fearful of praying for her meal that first night. Some witness she was. Still, she shuddered at the thought of everyone's reaction. "I'll tell the truth tonight at dinner."

"That's up to you, Becca. But I think it would be the right thing to do." Her grandmother squeezed Becca's hand then sat back in her chair. "Now, about Tate. I think he feels no one takes him seriously, that he has failed in so many arenas he doesn't deserve any respect. So he drowns his own feelings of worthlessness in the bottle. He has so much potential if he'd just let God use it."

"What about Shayna? She seems to love him."

"I think she does, but she's fed up with his drinking and shiftlessness."

"She seems to bury her dissatisfaction in shopping."

Gram nodded. "Poor child grew up with only one outfit each year, which she wore to school every day. I think she's determined never to let anyone pity her again."

Becca was certainly getting an eye-opening view of her relatives. "And Nick?"

Gram spread her fingers out palm up. "What can I say about Nick? He and Max are close, but I think each of them envies the other."

"What do you mean?"

"Their mother didn't stay long with Nick's dad, either, and took off when Nick was five. She doesn't so much as call on his birthday, but she recently began contacting Max again. So they both think their mom loved the other one best."

"Why Max and not Nick?"

Gram frowned. "I think Nick looks too much like his dad."

Becca's sympathies stirred. "Poor Nick."

Gram gave her a sharp look. "Be careful of wearing your heart on your sleeve. Nick is the type who might take advantage of you."

"He wants me to go to dinner with him."

"He might be fun as a friend, but no more. He's not ready to settle down, so be careful."

"What about Max? Is he good fun?"

"Max is salt of the earth. The things he endured with Laura would make your hair curl. But he stuck by her."

"He doesn't like me much."

"I think he likes you more than he wants to," was all Gram said.

So many undercurrents. How did she start to unravel everyone's true motives? Becca liked all the house's inhabitants. She didn't think any of them would be capable of murder. Maybe everyone else was right, and she was wrong. As Jake was prone to point out, she wasn't known for her common sense.

"Why the long face?" Gram asked.

"I was just wondering if I should give up. Maybe you're right, and it really was an accident."

"You follow your heart, my dear. You'll know when you're satisfied with what you've discovered."

Misty rubbed up against Becca's leg, and Becca picked her up and cuddled her.

"I'm surprised Max allowed you to bring your cat. He despises them."

"He about threw me off the porch when I showed up with her," Becca admitted. "But he was desperate enough for help that he finally gave in."

Gram rubbed the cat's ears. "Molly has begged for a kitten for over a year."

"So she said. She's adopted Misty."

"You'll be hard-pressed to take the cat when you leave." Gram's smile faded. "How long are you planning to stay? You've never said."

"I hope to stay all summer."

"I'll miss you when you go. I've already lost so much time with you."

"I'll be back often for visits now." Becca squeezed her grandmother's hand. "I think I've got these receipts organized. Now all I have to do is put them into the computer."

"I'll leave you to your work then. I think I'm ready for a nap." Gram stood and patted Becca's head as she went to the door. "I'll be down for dinner to give you moral support when you tell everyone who you are."

Becca flinched at the reminder of what faced her tonight. Max's reaction scared her the most. He'd said he hated falsehood. While she hadn't actually lied, she had bent the truth out of all recognition.

Gram was right though, the Holy Spirit had been taking her to the woodshed over her lack of total honesty. She had to be obedient and tell the unvarnished truth. She could only pray the fallout wasn't too extensive.

She worked steadily for two hours then glanced at the clock. It was after four. Just enough time to rest a bit before showering and changing clothes for dinner. She put away the folders and stood, stretching the kinks out of her back. All this paperwork was harder than she'd thought it would be. She wasn't used to spending such long hours hunched over a desk. Even when she was in school, she'd often taken her books and a blanket and studied on the lawn.

She went to her room. A vague aroma hung in the air. It reminded her of Max's cologne. Telling herself she was imagining things, she stretched out on the bed and rolled what she knew over in her mind. Gram was so certain none of the family could have wanted her parents killed. Who else on the island might be a suspect? A vision of Greg's handsome face flitted through her mind, but she pushed it away. He hated Max, but that had nothing to do with her parents' deaths.

What about Robert Jeffries—or even Mrs. Jeffries herself? But though Mrs. Jeffries filled Becca with distaste, there was no evidence to suggest she was anything more than a faithful servant to the family for twenty years. Becca sighed and sat back up. She might as well take a shower. Her mind was whirling too much to be able to rest.

She showered, redid her makeup then went to the closet for her purse. It wasn't on the shelf where she'd left it. Glancing around the room, she saw it on the floor beside the bed. Picking it up slowly, she realized someone had been in her room and had gone through her purse. She quickly checked, but her money was intact. Her driver's license was not fully back in the slot where it belonged.

Someone knew who she really was. Was it the person who had targeted her? Maybe he or she was merely looking for proof of their suspicions. Or it could be someone else who was suspicious of her. She remembered the scent in the room earlier. Max? She didn't want to believe he would hurt her, but why else would he be prying through her things?

She ran a brush through her hair, then went downstairs. It was time to face the music.

Wondering how he should let Becca know he had discovered who she really was, Max sat at the dining room table and waited for the rest of the family. His anger had cooled, but his determination to thwart Becca's plans had not. Gram surely knew Becca was her granddaughter. How had Becca convinced Gram to keep silent? Gram was a stickler for the truth.

The rest of the family filed in. Becca was the last to arrive. Dressed in a sky-blue dress, she looked good. Too good for Max's peace of mind.

"Whoa, you look way too pretty to stay home tonight," Nick said. "How about we go for a ride in the moonlight when dinner is over?"

"I need to buy some sticky notes. You can run me to the general store," Becca said. A blush stained her cheeks as everyone looked at her.

"I had something more romantic in mind," Nick said. "But if you insist."

"I think none of us are interested in your love life," Max snapped.

Nick held up his hands. "Okay, okay. Don't bite our heads off."

Max realized his tone had been too harsh. Becca was staring at him, and he wondered if she'd figured out he'd been in her room. He didn't see how she could, but the look in her blue eyes puzzled him.

"Let's eat. I'm starved," Shayna said. Her tone was cold and clipped.

Max figured she didn't like the attention Becca was getting. Shayna was used to being the center of male admiration.

Gram glanced at Becca. "Wasn't there something you wanted to talk about, my dear?"

Becca wet her lips and nodded. She cleared her throat then looked at the floor and frowned, clearly thrown off her intended statement.

"Has anyone seen Misty?" she asked. "She's usually underfoot at mealtimes, and I haven't seen her since this afternoon."

"I haven't, either, now that you mention it," Max

said. "She's usually rubbing up against my leg and making herself a general nuisance."

"You know you love her," Becca said.

Max tried not to notice the dimple in her cheek flashing. "Like a root canal," Max said. "Cats are a nuisance. She sheds hair all over me."

"Cats seem to know instinctively who dislikes them and go straight for them," Tate said.

"Fleabag," Max muttered. "I'll help you look. Maybe she got out."

"Oh, I hope not," Becca said. A worried frown crouched between her eyes.

They searched the house, but there was no sign of Misty. Max felt stupid calling for the cat he disliked.

"I'm going to look outside," Becca said.

"I don't see how she could have gotten out. There were no open windows or doors."

"Maybe she slipped out with a person."

"They would have seen her and told you," Max said. "Maybe."

Becca went in one direction, and Max searched the other way. There was no sign of the cat.

Becca felt frantic with anxiety. What could have happened to Misty? The island had wolves and foxes in residence, and Misty would make a tasty morsel for them. She had her claws, but they wouldn't be much use against a determined predator.

The sound of Max's voice calling for Misty faded as Becca pushed deeper into the woods. The light was fading, and she stumbled blindly along an overgrown path. She paused to catch her breath near a moss-covered tree that had been downed a long time. Her breath was loud in her ears, and she slowed her breathing to listen.

A mewl came from behind her. "Misty?" The mewl came again, and she followed the sound. She found her cat in a cage under the tree. She opened the cage and Misty jumped into her arms. She could feel her cat's heart pounding in her small chest. Who would terrorize her cat this way?

She suddenly realized it was done to lure her out here. She stilled her breathing and listened. Nothing. Then she heard something. A sliding noise, a rustling from behind her. She whirled. "Who's there?" she called.

Nothing answered but the wind. Prickles rose along her neck and spine. She forced herself to breathe in and out, though she wanted to bolt and run. There was nothing to be afraid of. Yet she *was* afraid. She couldn't explain why, but she suddenly knew the sound she heard wasn't some harmless animal, but something—or someone—focused on her.

The sound came again, and she realized it was the footsteps of someone trying to muffle their approach. "Who's there?" she called again, not really expecting an answer.

She shouldn't have come into the woods so far by herself. Max would have no idea where she was. A scream gathered in her throat, and she fought it back. Whoever it was wanted to terrorize her, but she had more backbone than to give in to fear.

A dark figure rose from the bushes, but it was too dark to make out features other than a huge headdress of some kind on the person's head. The figure brandished a wicked-looking blade.

She shrieked and bolted in the opposite direction, telling herself there was no such thing as a Windigo. Besides, she hadn't seen any big teeth. Clutching Misty to her chest, she dashed deeper into the forest and heard thrashing as the attacker followed.

She prayed as she darted through the trees and tried to figure out how to circle back to the house and still avoid the attacker. Her fear dropped away as she ran and anger took its place. She wasn't going to let him take her life the way he'd taken her parents'. She was going to bring this person to justice, no matter what it took.

The ground dropped out beneath her, and she tumbled down an embankment. She dropped the cat, and Misty yowled in protest then shot away into the dark. "Misty, no!" she called after the animal. She sprang to her feet and raced after her cat.

She found Misty crouched under a shrub then gathered her up and hurried toward the house.

She felt the attack before it came. A whoosh that she tried to jump away from. She almost made it, but the blade slashed through her arm. The darkness was complete, and she could make out only a vague form in the forest. She tucked Misty under her wounded arm then grabbed a stout stick on the ground and turned to face her attacker.

"I'm not going to make it easy for you!" she shouted. She jabbed with her stick, and she heard a throaty laugh. Following the sound, she thrust the stick with all her might and felt, then heard it find its target.

With a gasp, the figure fell back, and Becca took the opportunity to rush toward the house. She could see a dim glimmer of the outside light through the trees. She put on a last spurt of speed and broke through the tree-line onto the lawn. Glancing over her shoulder, she saw a figure following.

"Help!" she shrieked.

The figure stopped then ran toward her. She dropped the cat then turned to face the attacker again. The stick was wrenched from her hand.

"What do you think you're doing?" Max growled. He tossed the stick away.

"Someone tried to stab me." Becca could feel the warm trickle of blood on her arm, and she began to feel faint. She turned and spotted Misty nearby.

"Get Misty," she muttered, swaying on her feet. She had never fainted in her life, and she wasn't about to start now. If she passed out, Max would have to leave her where she fell. She was too big ever to pass as a dainty maiden in distress.

Could Max have been her attacker, and now he was trying to pass as her rescuer? She didn't want to believe it, but he always appeared at the most opportune time.

Her vision wavered even more. She caught a glimpse of Max's face as he rushed to catch her before she fell.

Chapter Thirteen

Max panted as he lugged a barely conscious Becca to the house. "I'm glad I worked out this morning," he muttered to himself. She was heavy.

"You're not supposed to notice," Becca whispered. Her hand was wrapped around his neck, but it loosened as she began to fade out again.

"I said you were a Valkyrie when you first showed up," he said. "I didn't expect you to wimp out on me. Come on now, stay with me."

In the yellowish light from the pole lamp, she looked half-dead. A smear of blood marred her cheek, and he felt the warm trickle of more on his hand from where it dripped off her arm.

He jiggled her when she failed to respond. "Who did this?" he demanded.

"The Windigo," she murmured. "Or maybe something else." Her lashes fluttered, then her eyes closed again.

She was delirious. She must have some kind of fixation about the Windigo. Panic flared when he saw how white she was. In the dark, he couldn't tell how serious her wound was. He had to get her inside and tended to.

He reached the back door and shouted for help. Her hand along the back of his neck tightened, and he found himself gazing into her eyes. Twin pools of blue that beckoned as much as the cold, refreshing water of Lake Superior. He wanted to shake her for scaring him half to death, but at least she was conscious again.

"Open the door!" He kicked it with his foot.

Mrs. Jeffries opened the door. "What on earth…" She held open the door while he carried Becca across the floor to the sofa and laid her down.

"Get me some soap and water and peroxide," he ordered. A little more color was showing in Becca's cheeks. She tried to sit up, but he pushed her back. "Lie still." He shoved up her sleeve and probed the wound. She winced. "Sorry," he said.

Mrs. Jeffries carried a basin of water to him. She had a bottle of peroxide tucked under her arm. "Want me to call the doctor?"

"No, I'm fine. I think it was just shock." Becca tried to sit up again.

"You are so stubborn," he said. "Lie still and let me tend to this." He cleansed the wound. "I think she'll be okay. It's not deep. Get me some tape." He poured peroxide on the cut. He winced when Becca's face went whiter and beaded with perspiration. If he ever got his hands on the madman who did this, he'd throttle him.

Becca gulped. "It's better now," she whispered.

"What happened?" he asked as he cut strips of white tape to make butterfly bandages.

"Someone had Misty in a cage, I assume to lure me out to look for her. He came at me with a knife."

"Could you see any features?"

"No, it was too dark." She looked around. "Where is everyone?"

Max looked around. He'd been so focused on tending Becca he hadn't noticed. "I don't know."

"Mrs. Baxter went to bed, and the young ones went out. Tate and Shayna had a fight, and they went different directions. Mr. Nick went for a walk along the beach."

Max didn't want to think anyone in the house would have tried to hurt Becca, but it had to be someone who had access to the house. Someone had taken Misty out. His gaze sought Becca's face again.

"Are you ready to tell me the truth yet?"

She flushed, but her gaze didn't waver. "I was going to tell you—all of you—tonight until we discovered Misty was missing." She glanced around. "Misty, where is she?"

"I brought her in," Mrs. Jeffries said. "She was yowling at the back door. She's eating." She pointed to the corner where Misty crouched over her dish of food.

Becca sighed and struggled to a sitting position. Her hands were visibly shaking, but Max hardened his heart. "I want to know the truth. Now." Though he knew the truth, he wanted to hear her say it. It would mean more if she told the truth. He hated liars.

"I'm Rebecca Lynn Baxter," she said simply.

"Becky?" Mrs. Jeffries said sharply. "No wonder you've been nothing but trouble since you got here. You always were one to go from one mess to another."

"That's enough, Moxie." Max fixed her with a stare, and the housekeeper pressed her lips together.

Tears flooded Becca's eyes at Moxie's harsh words. "I always knew you didn't like me," she said. She blinked and looked up at Max. "No one has called me Becky in years though. Everyone calls me Becca."

"You're here to find out what happened to your parents."

She nodded, and her lips trembled. "I know they were murdered."

Max was beginning to understand her motives. "It was an accident." He softened his voice. "I know it's hard to accept when something like that happens, but you have to face facts."

"Then why is someone trying to drive me away?" She held up her arm. "What about this?"

She had a point. "Has someone recognized you?"

"They must have. Only Saija Karola—Anderson—knows."

"Molly's friend's mother."

She nodded. "We recognized one another when I picked up Molly the other day."

"Could she have told someone?"

"Even if she did, it wouldn't explain why someone tried to roll the rock on top of me the day after I got here. Or the Windigo figurine on my bed." She shook her head. "Someone recognized me the day I arrived, and he wants to make sure I don't find out who killed my parents. But I'm not leaving until I do."

"Maybe it has nothing to do with your parents. Maybe the explosion really was an accident—a fortuitous one as far as the attacker is concerned. Maybe his main focus is on driving you away to keep you from inheriting. Everyone here stands to lose if your grandmother decides to leave you her money."

She was shaking her head even as he spoke. "I don't want Gram's money."

"The attacker might not know that." He wasn't sure he believed her. Who would turn down an inheritance if it was offered? Tate and Becca were Gram's grandchildren. They stood to gain the most, as did Becca's siblings.

And Tate stood to lose the most. If there were only one grandchild, he or she would inherit the bulk of the estate, including the house and property. Could Tate be behind this?

Max thought of his own daughter. He needed to protect Molly's interests, too. He pulled Becca's sleeve down. "There you go. I think you'll live."

"Thanks." She rubbed her arm. "We should call the sheriff and report the attack."

"I was about to suggest the same thing." Max went to the phone and dialed. The sheriff promised he'd be out to look around the woods, but Max knew the attacker was long gone.

A thought occurred to him. What if there *was* no attacker? Becca could have cut herself. The wound wasn't deep. Maybe she had done it to garner sympathy from Gram. She had to have known he was suspicious and figured this would be a way to dispel his disfavor and get Gram more firmly in her camp. Maybe *she* wanted the house and estate.

He wanted to reject that idea and believe Becca wasn't that devious. Looking at her sipping the tea Mrs. Jeffries brought her, he remembered the way she'd skirted any questions he'd asked. She hadn't been truthful with him. It made it harder to trust her now. The best he could do was withhold judgment and watch to see what she did.

The sheriff had come and gone after taking Becca's statement and promising to look into it. He'd never been the most ambitious of law personnel, seeming to prefer to let the Baxters handle their own issues. Becca ached all over. All she wanted was to crawl into bed and pull the sheets up to her chin. Reaction had set in, and she felt as if she was quivering inside. At least she knew it wasn't Max who had tried to attack her.

But did she? She watched him carefully over the rim of her teacup. They'd been separated. He could have doubled back and attacked her in the dark. She didn't know what to believe or who to trust.

God was always trustworthy. She knew God would help her untangle this mess. Faith in Him had brought her this far. But she wished she had an ally here in the flesh. She wanted to trust Max, but he had too much to gain by making her disappear. She would never do anything to harm Molly's future, but he didn't know that.

She put down her cup. "I think I'll go to bed," she said. She stood and staggered a bit as she turned.

"Let me help you." Max was at her side in two steps.

"I'm fine," she said.

"No, you're not. You've had quite a scare." His warm fingers closed on her good arm, and he steadied her as she went toward the back stairway. He walked her up the steps and down the hall to her room.

"Call me if you need anything," Max said.

He made no move to leave her, and his hand was still on her arm. Becca was certain he must be able to see the way her heart was beating. Her mouth was dry, and she swallowed. She knew she should just turn and open the door and go into her room, but she couldn't seem to make herself move.

His hand released her arm then traveled to her face. Gentle fingertips brushed across her cheek.

"You're really something, Becca. A scare like that and you came up fighting." His voice was husky. He ran his thumb across her lips then bent his head and brushed her mouth with his own.

The kiss was featherlight and brief, but the encounter left Becca breathless. She had to keep her distance from Max. He was away from the Lord, and he just might be a killer. She stepped back and opened the door. "Good night," she whispered.

She shut the door and leaned against it before he had a chance to answer. She listened in the dark until his muffled footsteps went down the hall. She went to her bed and prayed for strength and guidance. She needed all the help she could get.

Becca tossed and turned all night, her arm a throbbing pain that kept her from resting properly. She finally dozed off near dawn and awoke with the sun streaming across her face. Her arm still hurt, but the pain had dialed down a notch. She stretched and got up.

Today she was going to have to tell everyone the truth. She couldn't put it off any longer. Max knew now, and whoever had been targeting her knew, as well, so it might not come as a big surprise to very many people.

By the time she got downstairs to breakfast, the rest of the family had assembled in the dining room.

Her grandmother met her at the doorway. "You should have awakened me last night," she scolded. "How are you feeling this morning?"

"Okay. A little sore, but I'm all right."

She started toward the table, but Gram put her hand on her arm. "Do it soon," she whispered.

Becca glanced at her grandmother and saw an urgent

plea in her eyes. She gave a slight nod to Gram and went to the table.

"I'm going shopping on the mainland today, Becca. You want to come?" Shayna asked.

"She's not up to going anywhere," Max put in.

"I feel fine," Becca protested.

"In that case, you can join me in the office to do a little work." His voice brooked no argument.

Shayna made a face. "Slave driver."

"You can't go, anyway," Tate said. "I have to take the boat to town. I'm trading it on a new one."

Shayna clapped her hands. "A new boat! What are we getting?"

"A new sailboat," he said.

"A sailboat? I can't take that when I want to go to town!"

"You'll have to take the ferry."

"This is just another way to make sure you keep me here, isn't it? Well, it won't work." Shayna rose and rushed from the room.

Tate started to go after her, but Becca beat him to it. She hurried after the other woman and found her sobbing in the sunroom.

"I hate him," she said when she saw Becca. "He spoils everything."

"You know you don't hate him," Becca told her. She sat beside her on the sofa.

"Yes, I do. You don't know what it's like living with a man who wants to control every single thing I do. I hate my life. I wish I was dead!" Shayna buried her face in her hands and wept.

"God loves you, Shayna. He's there for you in all your problems."

"No, He isn't. No one is." Shayna turned and buried her face in Becca's shoulder. "My life is such a mess. I don't want to be married to Tate anymore."

"You guys can work it out. Why don't you go see the pastor at the church in town?"

"Tate would never agree to it. And besides, I don't love him anymore." Shayna pulled away and wiped at her eyes. She glanced at Becca, a calculating look that seemed out of character with her sadness. "I want Max."

Becca blinked, and a sharp pain of something she was ashamed to identify as jealousy shot through her. "Max?"

"He loves me, too. We're going to go away together."

Becca had known there was something there after hearing Tate warn Max off, but she'd hoped she'd misread the situation. "I don't know what to say."

"I'm only telling you this so you can avoid embarrassment. I've seen the way you've been throwing yourself at Max, and he's been mortified about it."

"There is nothing between me and Max," Becca said through stiff lips.

"Oh, I know." Shayna gave a tinkling laugh. "But I like you, and I don't want to see you hurt. Max likes to flirt. Poor thing, he can't help it. But it means nothing. He loves me."

The room felt hot. Suffocating. Becca rose. "I think I'll get some air," she said. She wouldn't cry. Not in front of Shayna. Escaping the room, she rushed out the door and around the corner of the manor to the garden. The cool serenity welcomed her, and she followed the path through the woods to the folly. She went to her favorite spot near the ruined fountain.

Sinking to her knees in the soft grass, she prayed for

God to take away the feelings she was developing for Max. This morning's reality check had been a hard one. She stayed in that position so long that when she finally tried to get up, her knees locked. Glancing at her watch, she realized she'd been out here nearly an hour.

Staggering to her feet, she heard a sound. Peeking over the top of the bushes, she stared into the brick ruins that were the far border of the folly. A man was backing out, looking around in a stealthy way.

Tate.

Becca watched him as he pulled the door shut behind him then walked confidently toward the house. What could be in those ramshackle ruins that would entice him to risk a broken bone or worse? Though Gram had always warned the children to stay out of the old ruined house because the walls could fall in at any time, they had played here anyway. She wouldn't risk it now. Over the years, some of the walls had crumbled even more. It looked much more dangerous than she remembered.

If Tate had gone in there, it must be safe for her to explore, as well. With a final regretful look at her watch, she knew it would have to wait. She was already late for work this morning.

If only there was a way never to see Max again. She didn't want to face him after the things Shayna had said. Did Max really feel she'd been chasing him? Becca's face burned. From now on, she'd be cool and distant, an ice princess. He'd soon see she had no romantic interest in him.

She'd known the minute she saw him he wasn't to be trusted. He looked dangerous, and he'd deliberately tried to get past her defenses. A thought struck her. Maybe he had flirted with her to try to discover who she was. He'd been using his charm to coax the truth out of her.

The thought made her mad, and she practically stomped to the office.

"I thought maybe you weren't going to show," Max said.

"I'm here. What do you want me to do first?" Her tone was clipped, but she didn't care. Let him wonder what was eating her. She'd endured his bad moods often enough.

"I'd hoped you were going to tell the others who you were this morning."

"I was going to, but—" She broke off. There was no way she was going to implicate Gram in anything.

Max shot her a quizzical look but didn't say anything else. He pointed to the desk. "I printed out the first five chapters, and I'd like you to go over them for continuity and accuracy of research. They're on your desk. If you like, you can take them to your room and rest while you read."

His kind tone almost melted the ice around her heart. Almost but not quite. She could still hear Shayna's earnest voice in her head saying her behavior had mortified Max.

She held on to her cool reserve. "I think I'll do that. You won't have to put up with my company that way." She grabbed the pages and sailed off as though she didn't have a care in the world.

Chapter Fourteen

Molly coaxed Max into going to church with Gram and Becca that weekend, and he discovered he was actually enjoying the sermon. He found himself watching Becca, wondering what made her tick. She intrigued him.

On Monday evening Max picked up Molly from town then got back to work. Becca had been prickly for two days, and he didn't know what to make of her. Maybe the kiss they'd shared the other night had rattled her as much as it had him. He wasn't sorry to see her pull away when all his senses were shouting for him to be cautious, as well.

Shadows were gathering in the twilight outside, and his stomach rumbled. Dinner was a little late tonight. Mrs. Jeffries must have been upset over something. Maybe her son had made another appearance and upset her.

He saved his file and stood, stretching his back muscles. Becca had given high praise to his chapters, and he'd plunged full speed into his work. He told himself he didn't care what she thought, but the reality was that her words of praise for his writing had meant more than she knew. She was different from anyone he'd ever met before. Maybe it was her faith. Watching her in church and at home had been a mesmerizing experience.

Mrs. Jeffries appeared in the doorway. She looked pale and somber. "Dinner is ready," she said in a monotone.

"Are you all right, Moxie?"

Her dark-eyed gaze flickered to his face then dropped again. "I'm fine."

"You seem upset."

"I said I'm fine!" she snapped, turning on her heels and stomping away.

Max shrugged and followed her. Maybe Robert had called wanting money again. That man needed something to shake him up and make him look at his life.

Everyone else was already in the dining room. Tate was swilling his liquor as usual, and Nick stood by the window talking to Shayna. Molly was chattering to Gram and Becca.

Max stood in the doorway and watched them all for a minute. His world revolved around the contact in this dining room, a small world. He remembered his college dreams to travel and see the world. Would his writing be better if he had expanded his horizons?

He'd traveled for a year right out of high school—France, Finland, Sweden—but he'd met Laura and settled here before he'd really experienced the world. Sometimes he wondered what he was missing, what Molly was missing. One of these days he would have to make a decision about the direction he wanted his life to go. He'd been drifting too long.

Becca glanced up and their gazes collided. The reserve in her face seemed to radiate dislike. Confusion made him frown. Had he been too hard on her in the office? He thought back to their last conversations and could see nothing that would have changed their relationship to the extent he saw in her face. Maybe she was afraid he was going to tell everyone who she really was, but he had no intentions of spilling the beans. She could tell the story herself in her own way.

He smiled to let her know she had nothing to fear from him, but she looked away, her expression still haughty. His lips tightened. Let her stew in a snit. It was nothing to him. Women were incomprehensible to him anyway, so it was just as well she was pulling away.

"Come sit with us," Gram called. "Your daughter is regaling us with tales of her escapades in town today. She's got your gift for storytelling."

Molly beamed at the compliment. "I'm going to be a writer like Daddy when I grow up."

"So what happened in town today?"

"Daddy, I already *told* you." Molly folded her arms across her chest.

The expression on her face reminded him of the one her mother had often worn when he was lost in his current novel's world. Some father he was. He gave her a guilty smile. "Sorry, baby girl, tell me again."

"You weren't listening, were you?"

"I'm sorry, I wasn't," he admitted meekly.

"We found a kitten nearly drowned in the water. I get to bring it home tomorrow."

"Whoa, did you really tell me that in the car?"

Molly nodded. "Uh-huh. You said fine."

Fine. Everyone was fine when he was lost in thought. "I hate cats."

"Becca brought her cat and you don't mind."

"I never said I didn't mind."

"Well, you tolerate her. You'll like Boo. He's really sweet. You *said* okay." Molly's face screwed up as if she was about to cry.

Max felt like the worst father in the world. He'd always told her "no cats," though. She should have known better than to ask.

"I told her it was all right, too," Gram put in. "We'll keep Boo out of your way."

"Cats never stay out of the way. They seem to know who hates them and they try to annoy me deliberately."

Becca laughed, and he found himself turning toward her. "You tell them, Becca."

"You won't get me on your side. I think you'll find out cats aren't nearly as bad as you think. Give Boo a chance."

"Would you just quit arguing? I've got a headache," Shayna said. "Let her have the stupid cat."

"It looks like I'm outnumbered."

"You are." Becca looked smug.

Max shrugged. "Okay. But the first time he claws the couch, he's out. Got it?"

"He won't claw anything. I'll watch him real close," Molly promised.

"We'll see. I never saw a cat that didn't claw the furniture."

"Misty doesn't. I got her a scratching post." Becca put her napkin on her lap as Mrs. Jeffries brought in the food.

"Maybe I'll make Boo one," Max said.

"Oh, Daddy, really?" Molly practically bounced in her chair.

"I'll see about it tonight," he promised. Maybe it would make up for not listening. He really needed to try to shake the habit of thinking about his characters even when he wasn't writing.

He grabbed the platter of roast beef, then glanced at Becca. "I suppose you want to pray first?"

She blushed and nodded. As he watched the color sweep over her cheeks, he realized he was developing feelings for her he never intended. At times she could be so shy and retiring and other times she was in-your-face bold. Sometimes she was a little girl, and sometimes far too wise and adult.

He bowed his head, and she prayed for the food in a firm, compelling voice. He found himself listening to the nuances in her prayer. She spoke as though she knew God intimately, as though he was an old friend she talked to all the time.

When Laura was alive, he and Gram used to debate about God. He'd even toyed with the idea of turning his life over to God. Maybe he was a coward, but it was hard to think about giving up control of his own life, of admitting he couldn't save himself. He couldn't shake the longing that gripped his heart as he listened to her final amen.

Tate choked on the gulp of liquor he sucked down at the end of the prayer, and it broke the holy hush that had fallen over the room. Max picked up the plate of beef and took some, then passed it to Shayna. Her hand lingered on his, and when he turned back around, he found an expression on Becca's face he didn't know how to read.

It almost seemed like—pain. Was she jealous of Shayna? Shayna was married. Not that she acted like it some days. But even if she seemed to have been absent the day morals were handed out, it didn't mean *he'd* fool around with a married woman. And if she thought he would, she didn't know him very well.

He turned back to his plate and scowled at his broccoli. Becca shuffled, and he glanced at her out of the corner of his eye. She licked her lips, and he thought she looked a little pale.

"I have something I want to talk to all of you about," she said. Her fingers twisted the napkin in her lap.

The conversations that were beginning to gear up quieted as everyone turned to stare at Becca. She took a sip of water. "I need to ask your forgiveness. I haven't been completely honest with you."

Ah, she was finally going to confess. He felt a little sorry for her when he saw her pale cheeks.

"You're really a preacher and not a research assistant, right?" Shayna asked with a grin. The amusement in her voice lightened the somber tone that had fallen over the room.

"We'd already guessed that," Tate said.

"Shut up, you guys, and let her finish," Max growled. He'd wondered when she was going to reveal herself to the rest of them.

"Yeah, I want to hear this," Nick said. He propped his elbow on the table and leaned his chin into his hand.

Becca bit her lip then drew a deep breath. "I haven't been honest about who I am. My name is Rebecca Lynn but there's more. It's Rebecca Lynn Baxter."

Silence greeted her announcement, then Tate leaped to his feet and threw his napkin on the floor. "Becky?

You're Becky Baxter? Cousin Becky?" His eyes were red from his drinking, but he looked sober enough.

"That's right, Tate." She nodded and stood.

"Why the big secrecy?" he demanded.

"I wanted to find out what had happened to my parents."

She said the words with such dignity, Max had to admire her courage. It couldn't have been easy for her. The last traces of his uneasiness about her motives began to trickle away. If she was revealing everything now, maybe he'd been wrong about her.

Tate looked as though he didn't know whether to hug Becca or slug her. He advanced around the table and stared down into her face. "Little Cousin Becky," he said. "You're all grown up. Our tree house is still out back."

"I know, I found it the other day," she said softly. "I wanted to tell you right from the beginning, Tate. We were friends when we were small."

He embraced her then. "We still are."

"Then you forgive me for the deception?" She returned his hug.

"Sure." He released her. "But I still don't get it. You could have come right to the door and asked about the explosion. You didn't have to sneak in."

"I wanted to find out the truth without anyone trying to spare my feelings."

"But why?" Shayna put in. "What's to know? The boat exploded. It was a terrible accident."

"Maybe. Maybe not."

Max was beginning to recognize that stubborn tilt to Becca's chin. The rest of the family would be just as incredulous as he'd been at the thought of it being anything but an accident.

"What are you saying?" Nick asked slowly. "You don't think it was an accident?"

"What?" Tate looked around as though dazed. "If it wasn't an accident then—"

Max glanced at his daughter. She shouldn't hear this. Before he could react, Gram rose. "I think Molly and I will take our dinner on the patio." She rose with her plate in her hand. "Come along, Molly."

Gram thought of everything. At least Molly wouldn't be in on the coming explosion. Gram and Molly carried their plates out the door.

Shayna stared at Becca. "No one would have wished Mason and Suzanne any harm."

"Oh, yeah? Their visit was *full* of fights and disagreements." Nick rubbed his chin.

"Oh?" Becca asked.

Max wasn't about to let the conversation go there. "He's exaggerating. Minor family spats, nothing more." He sent his brother a glowering look.

Nick ignored it. "Family spats? I don't know that I'd put them in that category, Max. Especially not that one you had with Suzanne."

Becca turned to stare at Max. "You argued with my mom?"

"It was nothing," he insisted. Heat scorched his face, and he sent Nick another warning look.

"Tell me," Becca said.

"Your mom had a way of getting around Gram," Nick said before Max could answer. "Max here was afraid she'd get Gram to cut Molly out of the will."

"It wasn't like that," Max protested. He cut a piece of his meat and popped it into his mouth, but it was tasteless to him.

"It's nothing to be ashamed of," Shayna said. "Max naturally wanted to protect Molly's interests."

Becca's blue eyes focused on Max, and his forehead broke out into a light sweat. He'd thought they were getting past this suspicion of one another. She already knew he wanted to protect Molly's interests, so why did she have to look at him with that shocked stare?

"You're making it out to be more than it was," he said. "I simply told her they'd been gone a long time, and Gram had other family to care about, as well."

Tate took a swig from his glass. "Give him a break. It's not like the rest of us didn't argue with them, too. Mason came waltzing in here like the proverbial prodigal son, expecting to be welcomed with open arms. Gram was happy to oblige, but too much time had gone by for the rest of us."

"And there was too much money involved," Nick said.

"That, too," Tate agreed.

"You *all* fought with my parents?" Becca was sounding bewildered.

"Yep. Even Gram," Shayna said. "I know you loved your parents, but they weren't perfect."

"They were to me," Becca said softly.

"Can we drop this subject? It's ridiculous to think any of us would have killed Mason and Suzanne," Shayna said. "And that *is* what you're saying, right? You thought one of us planted a bomb or something?"

"The police would have found that, but perhaps someone tampered with the motor."

Max felt the weight of four pairs of eyes as they all turned their gazes on him. "Why are you all staring at me?" he demanded.

Shayna was the first to look away. "It's just that your wife died the same way."

"I had nothing to do with it, and all of you know that."

"We know," Tate said. "Look, this is getting us nowhere. I'm glad you're here, Becca or Becky or whoever you are. For one thing, you've livened up a pretty dull existence."

"Call her Becca, she doesn't look like a Becky," Max said.

"What's a Becky look like?" Shayna asked. She tilted her head and looked at Becca.

"Not like a Valkyrie," Max said. He knew he'd said the wrong thing when Becca's eyes flashed, and she pointed her chin in the air.

"You can call me Becca," she said.

"No way. If I call you anything, it will be Brunhilde," he said, trying to get her to smile. It didn't work. She continued to glower at him.

"How nice you're having such fun at my expense," Becca snapped. "Now, back to my parents. What did you argue with them about, Shayna?"

Shayna raised her eyebrows. "Nothing really. I asked your dad if it was true you might be Will's only child."

Becca gasped, and it was all Max could do to hold in his own surprise. He had thought that old rumor had died long ago.

"Wha—what did my father say?" Becca whispered. The color leached from her cheeks.

Shayna shrugged. "He told me to mind my own business. But it's true, you know, Becca. No one knows for sure." She tilted her head. "You look a bit like that picture of Uncle Will."

"You're making things worse," Tate said. His nostrils flared, and he took another swig of his drink.

"I know, but I've seen pictures of Jake and Wynne. Becca doesn't look much like them."

"I know who I am," Becca said tightly.

"Do you?" Shayna asked. "Or do you just not want to know the truth?"

Becca's head reared back as though she'd been slapped. She whirled and ran from the room. Max started to go after her then stopped. What could he say? This might be a truth she had to face. No amount of self-denial could change facts. He'd heard all the rumors. And now that he knew what to look for, he had to wonder himself.

Chapter Fifteen

Becca's breath came hard in her lungs and she lunged up the steps and raced to her room. They were all hateful. Sitting there at the table discussing her lineage as though they were merely talking about the best type of tea to buy.

Becca wanted her mother. Suddenly everything she thought she knew about her life was like looking into murky water. Familiar landmarks were rendered strange and unfamiliar.

Who was she—really? When her grandmother had first mentioned the rumor, Becca had refused even to look at the facts. Now they had been forced on her. She peered at her face in the oval mirror above the dresser.

The features she'd seen all her life looked strange. She had never looked like her siblings. Both Jake and Wynne had brown eyes, hers were blue. Their hair was black as a raven's wing while her own shone with more gold and red than brown. She was nearly six feet tall, and Wynne was only five-three. Her limbs were long and gangly while even Jake, tall as he was, had a bulky build like their father.

His father, maybe not hers. Becca couldn't bear to think it might be true. She'd idolized her father. And would he treat her like his own if he'd suspected she belonged to his brother?

She cast her mind back to try to remember her uncle. Her memories were dim, but she thought he'd been quite tall with the same long, thin build she had herself. But did that prove anything? It wasn't uncommon for a niece or nephew to resemble an aunt or uncle.

A tap on the bedroom door interrupted her thoughts.

"Becca, may I come in?" Shayna's voice sounded anxious.

"Come in," Becca called.

The door opened and Shayna peeked in. "Are you all right? You ran off in such a hurry. No one meant to upset you."

"I don't believe any of this. I know who I am."

"Either way, you'd still be a Baxter."

"That's small comfort." Becca could feel all safety she'd thought she had in her life dissipating like a sinking swirl of seaweed. A rising panic squeezed her chest. Would her brother and sister still love her if the truth was something none of them were prepared to face?

"You look ready to run," Shayna remarked. She patted Becca on the shoulder. "This changes nothing."

"You're not the one living it," Becca retorted.

"True. But we all have things in our lives we have to live with." Shayna's lips had a bitter twist, and Becca wondered what secrets hid behind the smooth beauty of Shayna's face.

Shayna was staring at her with a strange expression on her face. "Why are you looking at me like that?"

"I was just wondering if you were right about your

parents' deaths. If someone really did kill them, then you would be even more a target if your father was your uncle Will. You'd be the only child of the oldest heir. Gram might think you should have the lion's share of the estate."

"I don't want any of it," Becca said. "Everyone seems to think this is about Gram's money, and I'm not here for that. I have a nice life on the mainland. I'm eager to get back to my friends and my school."

"I thought you were out of school."

"I am, but I'm enrolled for the master's program next fall." At school she felt safe. She knew what was expected of her, and the ivy-covered brick buildings gave her stability. All this uncertainty made her feel she was treading water over an unfathomably deep hole. She wanted to go back to paddling in the kiddy pool.

Shayna echoed Becca's own thoughts. "Maybe you should think about heading back to the mainland. I like you, Becca. I don't want anything to happen to you."

Becca shook her head. "You have no idea how much I want to do just that. But I'm going to find out what happened to my parents."

Shayna pressed her lips together. "Even if your father isn't really your father?"

"He *is* my father. He still loved me and cared for me just like he did Jake and Wynne. I loved him and I owe it to my parents to find out the truth and prove who I am."

"Okay. I'll help you if I can."

"You will?" Becca searched Shayna's face. She needed an ally, and the other woman's offer was like a life raft in the middle of a nor'easter, despite Shayna's cruel insinuations earlier.

Shayna nodded. "Why not? It will liven up the boredom around here. How can I help?"

"Sit down." Becca indicated the rocker by the window as she settled herself on the edge of the bed. "Who had the most to gain from getting rid of my parents?"

Shayna pursed her lips. "None of us were too excited to think about splitting the money another way. But we all knew we'd get our share, whatever it was, eventually. I still think you're not looking at it clearly. It really was an accident, Becca. I was here. I saw how upset everyone was when they died."

"None of you came to the funeral." That fact had bothered Becca more than she admitted. Not even Gram had come, and Becca resented that fact.

"Gram had a heart attack. She almost died, though she won't admit it. She just says she swooned." Shayna gave a wry grin. "She can put blinders on like no one else I know."

"I hadn't realized that was when it happened." The burden lifted a bit from Becca's shoulders. "I thought no one cared enough to make the trip."

"We were all hovering around Gram."

Becca said nothing, though the thought that they'd all gathered like vultures waiting for Gram to die made her shudder.

"Max and Tate were going to go, then Gram took another turn for the worse and they canceled their reservations." Shayna got up from the chair. "Speaking of Tate, he wants to go to town to a party, and I said I'd go with him."

"When are you going to leave him?"

"Who said anything about leaving?"

"You said you were in love with Max."

Shayna laughed. "But he's penniless. He's a fun diversion. I'll never leave Tate, at least not while Gram's still alive. Once she's gone and Tate has enough money that my half will let me live in the style I want, I might consider it."

Becca's burgeoning warm feelings for Shayna dissipated. "I see," she said stiffly.

"Don't go all high and mighty on me now," Shayna said, lifting her elegant shoulders in a shrug. "What else is there in life but to snatch the happiness we can while we can? I won't be young and beautiful forever. I need to think of the future."

"And what about eternity? You're planning for when men aren't chasing you anymore, but what about after you're dead?"

Shayna held out her palm to ward off Becca's words. "Don't start preaching now, Becca. If God loves me like you say, he would want me to be happy."

"No, he wants you to be holy," Becca said. "This life is a training ground for the life that lasts forever. Happiness is nice, but contentment in God is eternal."

Shayna blinked and she almost seemed to be listening. Then she shook her head. "Save it for someone else who will swallow that pap." She walked to the door. "See you at breakfast."

Becca wanted to say something to get through to her, but she knew it was useless. Only God could do the wooing. All she could do was try to live in such a way as to make others thirsty for the Living Water.

She washed her face and put a touch of makeup on to cover the redness around her eyes. She wasn't going to sulk in her room all evening. She was supposed to go to the movies with Nick tonight, and the thought of putting all this away for a few hours appealed to her. She pulled out her favorite dress, a red jersey knit that ended just below the knee and skimmed her figure. The neckline was demure, but the color brightened her mood.

Nick was watching a ball game when she stepped into the living room. His face brightened when he saw her. "I was about to come looking for you," he said. "I approve of the red dress." His gaze wandered over her figure then back to her face.

Her face burned. She should have chosen something less eye-catching. The last thing she wanted was to have to ward off Nick's attentions all evening. "Thanks," she said. "I should probably grab a sweater."

"Use Gram's mohair wrap. Shayna loves it." He went to the closet and pulled out a silver mohair shawl and dropped it over her shoulders.

Becca stroked it. "It feels like a kitten."

"It's yours," Gram said from the doorway. Her face was bright as she advanced into the room.

"Oh, no, I couldn't take it. It likely cost the earth," Becca said.

"I never wear it. Shayna wears it more than I ever did."

"Then you should give it to her." Becca started to pull it from her shoulders and hand it to her grandmother, but Gram put a firm hand over hers.

"No, I insist, Becca. I want you to keep it. It's nothing. You'll be inheriting much more than a silly wrap, anyway," she said.

"I don't want your money, Gram," she said.

"Perhaps not, but you have no choice. You will be my primary heir, Becca. My mind is made up."

Gram thrust her chin out in a way Becca was already

coming to recognize. "Please don't do that, Gram," Becca pleaded. Everyone already thought she'd come here to sway her grandmother into doing this very thing. Max would be certain she was a gold digger. She knew her grandmother was desperate to make up all that had gone wrong, but this wasn't the way.

"It's my money, and I can do what I want with it. I want you to have it. You've got a level head on your shoulders, Becca. I know you won't waste it or squander it. And you're a Christian. My decision is final." Gram patted Becca's arm. "Don't fret. You and Nick go out and have a good time. My lawyer should be here any minute." She glanced at her watch.

Becca realized there was no way she was going to talk her grandmother out of her chosen course of action. There was no law that said she had to take the money if it came to her. She could always make sure it got split up evenly. "All right, Gram. I'll see you later."

"Wow," Nick said when they were out of earshot. "You got through to the old lady really fast."

"I didn't want to get through to her, as you call it. I don't want her money."

"Maybe not, but you're getting it all the same. Think of the things you can do, the places you can go with that kind of money."

Becca could see Nick mentally rubbing his hands together. She pressed her lips together. "I'll just split it with the rest of them."

His eyes widened. "You wouldn't do that!"

"I certainly would. And I will if that's what she does."

Nick shrugged. "Let's not fight about it. The night is young and beautiful, and so are you." He slipped his arm around her and hugged her gently.

Becca wasn't used to flattery, and her face heated again. "Don't say things like that," she begged. "I know I'm not beautiful. You don't have to lie."

Nick laughed. "Are you nuts? Have you never looked in the mirror? You're gorgeous, Becca. Tall and regal, like a queen. You just light up a room when you walk in. I can't figure out why someone hasn't snapped you up already."

Becca tried to smile. She knew why he was lavishing her with flattery. He thought she'd be an heiress. Gram's announcement had spoiled any enjoyment of the evening she might have felt. Now she'd be weighing every word Nick spoke against his motives.

"I haven't been to see a movie in ages," she said.

"It will probably be one you've seen already," Nick said, steering the car expertly around the curves to town. "We only get old movies that are already on TV mostly. But at least it's a chance to get away from everyone else and eat some popcorn. It's something to do."

Nick's prediction proved correct, but Becca still enjoyed the old romantic comedy. She laughed until she cried and tried to forget her fears and worries. Making her way out of the ancient movie theater, she felt gloom begin to dampen her spirits again. Her task seemed overwhelming now. Who would trust her knowing Gram was giving her all her money?

"Becca!" Saija Anderson waved to her from the next aisle over.

Becca smiled and weaved through the crowd toward her friend. "I wish I'd known you were going to be here. We could have sat together." Her smile faltered when she recognized the man with Saija. Greg Chambers.

She introduced Nick to her old friend.

"Greg, this is my friend, Becca—ah—Becca Lynn," she faltered.

"It's okay, he told me you told him," Becca said. "And Greg and I have already met."

Saija's stricken face brightened. "Oh, that's right. I forgot you probably met my cousin when you were here when you were younger."

Becca's gaze met Greg's. His distant smile as he watched Becca made her feel like a mouse hiding from a hawk.

"We were reacquainted at the beach the other day," Greg said. "I've thought a lot about you over the years."

If he'd thought about her at all, it would have been as his cousin's friend and fellow pest. Becca knew he was lying. She'd been quite unremarkable as a child. "We'll have to get together for dinner one night," she said.

"You could come to our house," Saija said.

"That would be great. Where's your husband to-night?"

"He had to work late over on the mainland so he'll be gone until tomorrow. I was ready to get out of the house, so Mom took the kids to give me a break."

As they left Saija and Greg, Nick took Becca's arm. "Don't tell Max you saw him," he whispered.

"I know better," Becca said.

"Max still thinks he was responsible for Laura's death."

"I know. He found me at the beach with Greg."

"I bet that went over well."

"You could almost see the sparks flying between the two of them."

Nick laughed. "I'm sure. Greg hates Max, and the feeling is mutual."

"Do you think Greg had something to do with the explosion?"

He shrugged. "Who knows? The sheriff ruled it an accident. Max doesn't believe that though."

"Do you?" Becca pressed him, wondering why he was being evasive.

"We've hung out a few times. He seems an okay guy. Intense but okay. I think Max is just trying to find someone to lay the blame on. Maybe to get the focus off himself."

"So you think Max killed Laura?" Why was she so reluctant to believe that?

"Max is my brother." Nick flashed a smile. "I know he'd never hurt anyone. And I would never incriminate him."

"Are you saying you know something that would incriminate him if you told it?"

"You're putting words in my mouth. You should be asking Max these questions." He smiled. "Enough of serious things. Let's enjoy our drive home and forget about stuff like murder and mayhem."

It was more what he wasn't saying that alarmed Becca. She managed a smile and chatted about her schooling all the way home.

Nick parked in front of the house then killed the engine and leaned back in his seat. He slid his hand along the top of Becca's head and leaned toward her.

Her mouth went dry, and she fumbled for the door handle and quickly opened it. "I'd better get inside." She saw him start to reach for her and slipped from his grasp.

He frowned, and she heard him sigh loudly, but he didn't complain, though he slammed the car door more loudly than necessary.

"Looks like everyone is up," Becca said, walking ahead of him. Nearly every window blazed with light.

He caught up with her and took her arm. "Are you afraid of me, Becca?"

His fingers on her arm made her feel panicked but she fought it. "Not at all. I just thought I should get in and check on Gram."

"She's fine. Let's take a walk in the garden."

"I'm really tired," she said. She wanted to tug her arm from his grasp but refrained.

"I've been wanting to get you to myself for days," he said. "I'm going to woo you, Becca. You're the woman I've been waiting for."

"Me or the money?" She blurted the words before she stopped to think.

His grasp slackened. "That was uncalled-for. I asked you out before I knew who you were."

"That's true," she admitted. "I'm sorry. I'm just so confused by everything right now. Let's put off serious discussions for the moment, okay?"

"You sure you want to face the gauntlet? Gram probably announced her intentions to the family and they're all plotting how to get their share." Nick grinned and turned to start to the house.

Relief flooded Becca at his acceptance of her reticence. She liked Nick, but only as a friend. She didn't think she could ever feel more than friendship for him. And she didn't trust that his interest was in her and not in Gram's money.

At the bottom of the steps to the porch, he paused

and pulled her toward him. His fingers touched her chin and tilted her lips up to meet his. Becca tried to draw away, but his hands held her trapped.

"Nice night." Shayna's voice caused Nick to jerk away.

He turned and his hand dropped from Becca's chin. "I didn't see you skulking in the shadows," he said.

Shayna got up from the porch swing. "I wasn't skulking. Sorry to interrupt your romantic moment." Her voice was caustic, and she walked in angry, jerky movements to the front door. "Carry on."

Becca used the interruption to escape. "Thanks for a wonderful evening, Nick," she said, hurrying up the porch steps. "I'd better go check on Gram."

Chapter Sixteen

Max pretended not to notice Becca come rushing inside with her lipstick smeared and her face flushed. He tried to stifle the feelings of jealousy that rose to choke him. He failed. Gritting his teeth, he tried to recapture his thoughts on his manuscript, but it was no use. He'd lost the muse.

The rest of the family sat around the living room. Gram was knitting in her chair, Molly's new kitten playing with a ball of yarn at her feet. Shayna had come in a few moments ago, but she was morose and grim as she flipped through the channels on television. Tate was in a near stupor on the couch. A normal evening at the Baxter house. Luckily, Molly was already in bed.

Becca rushed upstairs then Max heard her door slam. Moments later Nick came inside. A tiny spot of lipstick was at the corner of his mouth. Max found his gaze drawn to it. He simultaneously wanted to throttle his brother and quiz him at the same time. He controlled himself.

"Fun evening?" he asked casually.

"It was okay. Did you tell them all the news?" Nick asked Gram. He walked past Max and dropped onto the couch next to Tate.

"What news?" Shayna's frown eased as she looked up.

The click of the knitting needles stopped then resumed at an even faster pace. "I did not," Gram said. "But now that you're all here, I might as well. I've decided to leave Windigo Manor to Becca."

There was a collective gasp from all parties in the room. Max curled his fingers into his palms. "What about Molly?" he asked.

"You'll all have a share," Gram said. "Molly, too. But Windigo Manor should go to the eldest Baxter. Will was my eldest son, so his child should inherit the house and enough money to keep it up."

"You don't even know if she *is* Will's daughter!" Shayna moved restlessly.

"I've seen enough to believe it," Gram said. "Her mannerisms are very like Will's, and she looks like him. The longer I've watched Becca, the more I'm convinced."

"She could look like him and still be his niece and not his daughter," Tate said, rousing enough to take part in the discussion.

"You should think about this," Shayna said. "Tate and I have been here for you all these years. Becca has been here two minutes. It's not fair!"

"I agree." Becca stood in the doorway. Her face was pale and set.

Max noticed the strain around her mouth. "So you got what you came for. I hope you're pleased." He couldn't keep the disgust from his voice.

"I don't want the house or the money. I told her that." Becca swallowed, and the long line of her throat moved. Then she shivered as though cold. "I can't live here, Gram. I have school to finish." There was a pleading note in her voice.

"You can come back when you're done," Gram said.

"I'm not Will's daughter!" Becca sounded near tears.

Max found it hard to squelch the sympathy for her that kept rising in his chest. Maybe she hadn't planned it. She seemed so innocent. He reminded himself of how Laura could appear the same way.

Gram's face softened with love. "Whoever is your father, you're my own dear granddaughter, Becca. I've seen the spirit you have, the tender love in your heart, and you love God. Those are all the very qualities I want for the person who is fit to care for Windigo Manor for future generations."

Tears sparkled on Becca's lashes. "You haven't seen Jake or Wynne in years. They're more qualified than me—especially Jake. Wait until you meet them."

"What am I—chopped liver?" Tate slurred the words and staggered to his feet.

Gram sighed. "Tate, you've had too much to drink. Let's discuss this in the morning."

Tate made a sweeping motion with his arm and almost fell. "We'll discuss it now," he shouted. "I've served you faithfully for years, and this is the thanks I get?"

"You tell her," Shayna muttered. She crossed her arms over her chest and glared at Gram, then at Becca.

"It's about suitability," Gram said. "I love you, Tate, but you'd have this place mortgaged within a year to fund your drinking and gambling."

"I don't gamble," he protested.

"You lost fifty thousand dollars last week, so what would you call it?"

"Playing the stock market. There are always risks."

"But you seem to seek out the riskiest propositions out there," Gram said. "You haven't shown me you can handle money. I'm sure the amount I'll be leaving you will be gone in weeks. I'm sorry, but this is the way it has to be."

Max wanted to protest but he knew it would do no good. Then Gram looked at him.

"You could have handled the estate with great skill and dedication, Max. But you're not my own flesh and blood."

"Molly is," he reminded her. His chest felt tight.

"She is," Gram agreed. "And I love her dearly, you know that. But I must do what's right, and I think this is the right thing for all of us."

"Why are we even talking about it?" Becca asked. "You're going to live many more years, Gram. We won't have to worry about this for a long time. By then Molly may be grown up, and you can leave it to her."

"I know you'd all like to think I'm invincible, but these past few months have clearly shown me how fleeting life really is," Gram said. "I hope to be around to dandle great-grandchildren on my knee, but I'm nearly eighty. And days like today I feel every minute of that time."

"Don't talk like that." Becca went to her grandmother and knelt by her chair.

Gram smiled and patted her face. "See what I mean? You have a heart that yearns to help, Becca. That's a rare thing. You'll care for Windigo Manor." Her hand dropped to her side, and she stood. "I'm tired. I'm going to bed. Remember I love you all, and no one will be left out of the will. You'll all have your share." She patted Becca's head then left the living room.

Becca slowly rose then sat in Gram's vacated chair. "I suppose you all hate me now," she said.

Max watched her as her lips trembled. She was a good actress. Really good. Even Tate seemed taken in by her.

Tate's face softened as he watched her, and he leaned forward. "Hey, if it can't come to me, I'm glad it's you, Becca. And you'll never toss me out on my ear, right?"

Becca smiled. "Of course not, Tate. We're family." She pushed her hair away from her face. "Oh, why are we talking like this anyway? Gram is going to live a long, long time. And I'm going to prove I'm Becca Baxter, daughter of Mason and not Will."

"I don't see how you can prove that," Max said. "You heard Gram. She's convinced. With all parties concerned dead, there will be no proof."

Becca paled further and she looked down at her hands. "I can try," she whispered.

"Well, I, for one, think Gram made a good choice," Shayna said.

Max glanced at her in surprise. He'd thought she would raise more of a fuss than that.

Shayna saw his expression. "What, you think I can't see Becca is real quality? I admit I was angry for a few minutes, but there is plenty of money to go around. I'm convinced she's not lying now."

Becca's eyes widened. "You thought I would lie about that?"

"You lied once," she pointed out.

Becca's lips tightened. "And I confessed. I could have kept my mouth shut."

"Gram was sure to leak it as soon as you told her," Max said.

"She recognized me!"

"I'm not doubting you're who you say you are. I saw your ID. Though I guess you could have forged that."

"I didn't forge anything. I'm telling the truth."

"So you say." Max wasn't sure why he was goading her like this. He didn't doubt she was really Rebecca Baxter. The truth was obvious. Now. But he didn't like her initial evasions.

She swallowed and looked away. He didn't know why he liked looking at her so much. She was striking in a way that made it hard to ignore her as he wanted to. High cheekbones and a riveting smile.

"Lay off her, Max," Shayna said sharply. "You can make someone bleed with that tongue of yours. She's entitled to Gram's estate. More so than you and I."

"I can't take any more of this. I'm just going to bed." Becca got up and went toward the doorway.

Max knew he should apologize. Gram could leave her money to anyone she wanted. But the words stuck in his throat. Becca's coming had robbed his daughter. It would be hard to forgive her for that.

Becca wasn't crying by the time she got to her room. She was mad, furious, in fact. She hadn't asked for any of this. All she'd wanted was to find out what had really happened to her parents. Now here she was, not even sure who her father was, hated by the rest of the family, regarded as a traitor by a man she was beginning to suspect she could love.

"*I hate this, Lord,*" she said petulantly. She grabbed

a pillow from the bed and clutched it to her chest before sinking on the floor. *"None of this has turned out the way I thought it would."*

So who had killed her parents? Fate? Or did a murderer lurk behind some smiling face she had grown to trust? She didn't believe any of them were capable of cold-blooded murder. Maybe she should just give up and go back to school.

No. She wasn't going to quit this time. She was done with quitting. Giving up was why she was still in school at age twenty-five. She changed majors so many times Jake had jokingly called her a jack-in-the-box instead of a jack-of-all-trades. Maybe he was right. She'd hopped from goals so many times, she'd lost count. But this was too important to mess up. She would stay the course.

But only if God helped her. It was too hard to do on her own, and she realized that was what her problem had been. She was trying to prove she could do it instead of leaning on Him. He could give her the strength to see this through.

She got into her pajamas and crawled under the covers. A bloated moon shone through the window. She read her Bible then turned out the light. Lying in the dark, she prayed for strength of purpose and for God to show His will for her life. Maybe she was *supposed* to be caretaker for this property. She wanted to be open to what God had in store for her. She finally drifted to sleep.

She was underwater. Seaweed wrapped around her neck, choking her. She fought the long green strands, tugging on them with all her might as she struggled for breath. The cold water of Lake Superior numbed her limbs, and she flailed against the creeping paralysis.

The seaweed became a pillow pressed against her face and a hand on her throat. Becca couldn't see her assailant, but came awake and began to fight with all her might. She struggled against the muffling folds of the pillow. Her thrashing wrapped the bedclothes around her in a tight embrace, but she managed to get one leg free and kicked out with her right foot.

The pressure on her throat lessened a fraction, and she flung out an arm, connecting with someone's face. She felt whisker stubble, then the pillow fell away, and a dark figure dashed from the room. Sick and shaken, she rolled onto the floor and lay there. She drew air in past a sore throat and rubbed her neck.

She should call for help, but she knew she'd never get more than a squeak out past the pain. Rocking to her hands and knees, she retched weakly, but nothing came up. Sucking in her breath, she tried to slow her racing heart.

She grabbed the edge of the bed and managed to get to her feet. Her legs trembled and she swayed as she walked toward the door. Max. Becca wanted Max. His strength and calm assurance. He would know what to do.

Holding to the wall, she wandered down the hall and rapped on his door. There was no answer. She knocked again a little louder. When there was still no response, she twisted the doorknob and stumbled into the room.

"Max?" Flicking on his light, she saw his bed was empty.

She leaned against the doorjamb, not sure she could stay standing. Could Max have been her attacker? She didn't want to believe that, but Molly had the most to lose through Gram's decision. If Becca were out of the way, Molly would get a full share with everyone else.

"Becca? What's going on?" Max stood behind her, still fully dressed, his hair rumpled. Was he disheveled from the struggle with her? Heartsick, she wobbled where she stood.

"What's wrong?"

"S-someone tried to kill me," she rasped out.

His face changed from mild concern to amusement. "Were you dreaming?"

She tilted up her chin to expose her throat. "Does this look like a dream?"

His face darkened, and he examined her neck, touching it with gentle fingers. She flinched, and he sucked in his breath. "Who did this?"

"I don't know. Where were you?" She winced at the accusation in her voice.

He scowled. "Molly woke up with a nightmare as I was going to bed, and I lay down with her for a while."

That explained his rumpled appearance. Maybe. Becca wanted to believe him.

"Show me," he said. He took her arm and helped her back down the hall.

In spite of her suspicion, Becca couldn't help feeling better as she clung to his arm.

He flipped on the light in her room. Her bedclothes were in a heap on the floor where she'd left them, and one pillow was beside the bed.

"I woke up with a pillow over my face and someone choking me," she whispered.

"Man or woman?"

"Man. I felt whiskers." Becca glanced at Max's face and examined the whiskers on his face and chin.

"Quit looking at me like that!" he snapped. "You have to know I wouldn't hurt you, Becca."

She wanted that to be true. She nodded. "Okay, but you have to admit it looks suspicious."

He didn't answer but strode forward and grabbed the blankets from the floor. Tossing them onto the bed, he glanced around the room.

Becca saw something at his feet. "What's that?" she asked, joining him in the middle of the room. She knelt and grabbed a familiar fountain pen. She turned it over to reveal the initials *M.D.* Max Duncan.

She remembered when she'd first come here and he wouldn't let her use this pen. No one used it, he'd said. Something squeezed at the hope she'd nurtured. "I think this is yours," she said.

He glanced to the pen in her hand. "My pen. How did it get in here?"

"You tell me." Tears burned the back of her eyes. "I'm going to call the sheriff." Expecting him to leap toward her, she backed away from him toward the phone on the dresser.

"I'm not going to attack you," he said.

His face softened with a plea she had to steel her heart against.

"I don't know how my pen got in here, but obviously someone wants to implicate me in this attack. Call the sheriff." He held out the phone.

Becca snatched up the phone and dialed. When the dispatcher answered, she told her what had happened, and the woman said a deputy would be out in a few minutes.

"It wasn't me," Max said when she hung up the phone.

"Then how did your pen get here? You always have it in your pocket. You wouldn't even let me borrow it in your office."

"Someone must have taken it." He patted his pocket. "I didn't realize it was missing. Surely, if I'd attacked you, I'd have a better story made up."

Oh, how she longed to believe him. She felt hurt and shattered inside by his betrayal. One minute he'd kissed her and the next he'd tried to choke her. Was he some kind of psychotic?

He took a step toward her, and she shrank back. Consternation filled his face. "Becca, you're killing me."

He was the one trying to murder someone. She held out a hand to ward him off. "Don't come any closer or I'll scream."

He stopped and shook his head. "I can't believe this," he muttered.

"What's going on?" Gram stood in the doorway, her robe belted around her ample figure. She blinked sleepily.

"Someone tried to choke Becca. The sheriff is on his way. She thinks I tried to kill her."

"Oh, my dear, are you all right?" Gram stepped into the room and put her arms around Becca.

Becca burst into tears and buried her face against her grandmother's shoulder. "I'm scared," she sobbed. "I want to go home. I want my mother."

Gram patted her shoulder. "There, there. We'll get to the bottom of this. I'm sure it wasn't Max who tried to hurt you, but we'll figure it out."

Why would no one believe her? The proof was still clutched in her hand.

Her hand.

She dropped the pen on the floor. "I shouldn't have touched it," she said. "The sheriff will want to dust for fingerprints."

"It was likely someone who broke in and took Max's pen to implicate him."

Becca knew she'd find no ally in Gram. She wouldn't want to believe anyone in the house could be guilty of attempted murder. But the stakes had been raised by Gram's announcement, and Becca knew it would take a miracle to live long enough to collect any inheritance.

Chapter Seventeen

The sheriff had taken Max's favorite pen in for fingerprints, though he'd muttered something about it likely
being an attacker from the village.

Max couldn't blame Becca for being suspicious, but
it hurt all the same. The evidence seemed overwhelming. It would have been the easiest thing in the world
to have lost the pen during a struggle with Becca.

But he hadn't been there. He curled his fingers into
the palms of his hands. Becca was in danger, and he
needed to do something about it. How could he, though,
when she suspected him of the murder attempt? The
helpless feeling made him feel caged.

The entire household was still assembled in the living room. Was it his imagination or did everyone look
at him with suspicion? Molly rubbed her eyes and
leaned against his chest.

"Let's get you to bed, baby girl," he said. He stood,
cradling her against his chest. "I'm bushed. I'll see all
of you tomorrow."

"How can you think about sleeping at a time like

this?" Shayna demanded. "Who knows if someone will creep back in and murder us all in our beds?"

"I think you're being melodramatic," Max said dryly. "Becca seems to be the target. And I need to figure out why."

"Isn't it obvious?" Tate sat slumped in a chair by the window. "Someone really did kill her parents, and whoever it is doesn't want her to discover his identity."

"I don't believe that," Nick said. "I still think it was an unfortunate accident." He shot a glance toward Becca. "Sorry."

"Then why is someone trying to kill Becca? You're not making sense, Nick." Max shot his brother a quelling look.

Nick shrugged. "Yeah, I guess so." He ruffled his hair and slumped back in his chair.

Becca looked pale but composed. Max had to admire her spirit. She'd answered the sheriff's questions with quiet composure. Her bruised throat looked sore, and he wanted to throttle whoever had hurt her like that.

His gaze wandered around the room. Someone didn't want Becca to inherit Windigo Manor.

Mrs. Jeffries wandered in; her housedress was wrinkled and its collar askew. "I heard the Windigo tonight. I knew something bad was going to happen. Maybe it was the Windigo himself that attacked you," she told Becca.

Becca flinched and wrapped her arms around herself. "I don't think so, Mrs. Jeffries. God wouldn't let a demon harm me."

"It's just a superstition," Shayna said.

"There are demons in the world," Becca said. "But they can't harm a Christian. I'm not afraid." She said the words with a hint of defiance, and Max admired her spirit.

"I'm not nearly as worried about some mythical creature as I am about a flesh-and-blood person who is targeting Becca." Molly was asleep by now, and he cradled her gently.

"You'll see," Mrs. Jeffries said with a sniff. She dropped the tray of tea onto the coffee table with a clatter and stalked out of the room.

"You've offended her," Gram said.

"She's getting worse," Max said. He stared after the housekeeper. Could Mrs. Jeffries be behind this? Maybe she was upset about Gram leaving the house to Becca. He resolved to feel her out tomorrow sometime and see if she harbored any animosity toward Becca.

"See you in the morning," he said, carrying his daughter out of the room and up the stairs. He put her into bed then stood looking out her window at the moon shimmering on the lake.

He saw a figure flit between the trees. An animal? He stared through the gloom but didn't see any more movement. He turned and exited Molly's room and went down the back stairs through the kitchen and out the back door.

The dew hung heavy in the air, and pine scent wafted to his nose as he trod over evergreen needles into the woods.

Once in the woods, he stopped and cocked his head, listening for any sounds other than crickets and the wind soughing through the treetops. Nothing.

Maybe it had been his imagination. He retraced his steps to the house and went inside. He found Becca in the kitchen putting her cup into the dishwasher.

She flinched when she saw him and started to turn toward the door.

"Becca, wait," he said.

He could see her visibly shrink as he approached her where she stood by the sink. "It wasn't me in your room tonight," he said urgently. "I want to help you figure it out. I don't want anything to happen to you."

"At least not until your manuscript is done, is that it?"

Her caustic tone stung. "That's not it at all! I—I care about you. I admit I'm flat-out scared that this is more than we think it is."

"*You're* scared? What about me?"

He put his hands on her arms, and she didn't pull away. "Let me help you. I thought maybe there was something developing between us, Becca, something special."

"I did, too," she admitted. Her blue eyes searched his face.

"Don't let unfounded suspicion destroy it," he whispered. His right hand trailed up her arm. She flinched as he touched her neck. "I'd like to kill whoever did this to you."

Her eyes widened, then he leaned closer and kissed her, relishing the taste of her, the scent of her perfume.

She held herself stiffly at first then returned his kiss. He held her close then buried his face in her fragrant hair. "Let me help you," he whispered again.

She pulled away. "It really and truly wasn't you in my room tonight?"

"I swear it wasn't, Becca. Get a Bible and I'll take an oath on it."

"I believe you," she said. Her hand stroked his cheek. "Actually, I don't think he was quite as scruffy as you are tonight."

Her hand was soft and warm, and he pressed his cheek against it. "I want to keep you safe. Let me walk you to your room." He had to let go of her soon, or he wouldn't be able to walk away.

It had been so long since he'd felt such tugging toward a woman. The emotions he'd felt for Laura had been youthful infatuation. When he'd finally seen her real personality, Molly was on the way. What he felt for Becca was different. He admired her as a person first, her integrity and determination. What did she feel for him? He didn't think he was ready to find out yet.

She went ahead of him up the back stairs and down the hall to her room. "Good night," she whispered, staring up at him.

He wanted to kiss her again but stepped back instead. "In the morning we'll see what we can discover about all this. Call me if you need me."

"I will." She stepped inside the room and flipped on the light then shut the door.

He went to his room and undressed. Lying on the bed, he felt a sense of hope he hadn't experienced in a long, long time.

The next week passed with Becca on tenterhooks. She spooked at every sound and shadow and tried never to be alone. Max's gentle attention was like water on a parched garden as he escorted her to church and followed her around in the evenings.

On Monday morning, Becca woke to the sound of birds chirping. She rolled over and looked at the clock. Nearly nine o'clock! She'd be late for work. She quickly showered and rushed downstairs.

The house felt empty. She wandered through the dining room and saw Shayna and Tate on the back patio. She stepped outside and lifted a hand in greeting. "Where is everyone?"

"Gram went to town with Nick. She wanted to stop at the store for something. I think she just wanted to get out for a while," Tate said. "Max took Molly out to the graveyard. Today is Laura's birthday, and Molly wanted to take flowers to the grave."

"That's sweet." Becca snagged a cinnamon roll from the tray in the middle of the table then poured herself a cup of coffee.

"What's on your agenda today?" Shayna asked.

"I want to work on Max's notes then tackle the last of Gram's filing. I'm about done with inputting everything into the computer."

"Anything I can do to help?"

Becca shook her head. "Thanks, but I've got it under control. What are you going to do today?"

"I might go to the mainland. My spa is having a special, and I desperately need a facial." Shayna rubbed at the side of her face. "This wind is so drying. Tate is going along. He has some business to attend to."

Becca wished she could get away from her worries for a while. But she had work to do. She finished her roll and went to the office. Since Max was gone, she decided to work on Gram's work first. She pulled the last stack of papers to be filed out of the drawer and began to sort them into piles.

Halfway into the stack, she ran into an envelope. My darling, it said on the outside. Was it to Max? Her hand hovered over the flap. She knew it was none of her business, but maybe it was related to her parents' deaths. With a decisive flip, she opened it and pulled out the single sheet of paper. Her gaze traveled over the flamboyant writing. It was signed by Laura.

Who was it written to? She glanced at the beginning. My darling, it said. Max or the man she'd been seeing? Intrigued, she began to read:

My darling, I can't tell you how eager I am to be with you always. Soon this boring life on the island will be a thing of the past. I know you'll love San Francisco. We'll meld into the crowd and no one will ever find us and drag us back here again.

But we must be careful. Max suspects something, and if he discovers our plans, I don't know what he'll do. Something drastic. He'll stop at nothing to make sure I'm miserable.

He was staring at me last night, and I could almost swear I saw murder in his eyes. So be careful, my darling. Next week we start our new life. Yours forever, Laura.

Her hands were shaking. Becca rubbed her slick palms against her jeans then fumbled as she put the letter back into the envelope. Had Max killed Laura? She was frightened of him. Had he seen this letter or had Gram found it and stashed it here?

Becca wanted to believe the tender kisses he'd given her, wanted to trust the honesty she saw in his eyes. But it might get her killed. All the bright hope she'd felt growing this past week seeped away.

She was living in a fairy tale. Max couldn't be ruled out of the equation. The most she could do was stay on her guard and try to sniff out the truth.

She stuck the envelope back into the drawer and

pulled up the financial program on the computer. By the time the morning was over, she'd put the last of the receipts in the computer.

Gram came in. "You work too hard," she scolded. "Every time I see you, you're working on something. Max is gone. Why don't you take it easy this morning?"

Becca managed a smile. She wanted to ask her grandmother about the letter she'd found, but the words stuck in her throat.

Gram leaned over and touched Becca's throat. "The bruises are fading. How does it feel?"

"Still a little sore but okay." Becca pushed away from the desk. "I got your books in order." She told her grandmother the balances in the various accounts.

A look of distress crossed Gram's face. "Are you sure about the balances?" she asked slowly. "I rarely look at the books. Max takes care of all that, but I thought—" She broke off and looked away.

"Yes, I connected to the Internet to balance the books. It's totally up to date."

"I see." Gram seemed pale as she turned to go. "I think I'll lie down awhile."

"Is everything okay?" All thoughts of confronting Gram about the letter faded as Becca eyed her grandmother's pallor.

"Fine, fine," Gram said. "I'm just a little tired." She patted Becca's arm then went out the door and up the steps.

Becca tidied up the desk and grabbed her pen as Molly came running into the room. "Hi!" she said.

Becca turned to face her. "Did you have a nice morning?"

Molly nodded. "We took flowers out to my mother's

grave. Dad promised we could make cookies this afternoon. Want to help us?"

Becca was conscious of Max's presence as his broad shoulders filled the doorway. "Your dad is going to bake cookies?"

"Hey, you don't think I can do it?" He flexed his muscles. "Come along, and let me show you how a real man bakes cookies."

Becca laughed and got up from her perch on the chair. "Aren't we working?"

"Not today. I'm lazy, and I need to spend a little time with my daughter." He stepped aside to allow Becca through the doorway. "Lead the way to the kitchen."

She went down the hall with Molly's hand in hers. Mrs. Jeffries scowled when they invaded her kitchen, but she merely muttered and got out of the way when Max told her what he'd planned.

Max took an apron from the hook and dropped the loop over his head then tied it on in back. He found a smaller one for Molly while Becca grabbed the red one just like his.

"Now you need a chef's hat," she said.

"I never figured out why they wore those tall hats," he said. "I'd be worried it was going to drop off into my baking."

Molly giggled. "I want to make chocolate chip cookies." She pulled the large tin of sugar toward her. "I get to measure!"

"Hold your horses," her father told her. He got down a large stoneware bowl and rummaged in the cabinets. "I know there have to be chocolate chips in here somewhere."

Becca went to the pantry and found them beside the cake mixes. "Here they are." She put the bag of chocolate chips on the counter beside Molly.

Molly picked them up and started to dump them in the bowl. "Hold on," Max said. "You're rushing me. This takes time and finesse. A master chef cannot be hurried."

Molly huffed but settled back to watch her father get out the sugar and butter. "I want to measure," she said again.

"Fine." Max pushed the measuring cup and butter toward her.

She cut the butter carefully along the line and dumped it in the bowl.

Watching them work together, Becca hid a smile. Max looked completely at home in the voluminous apron with his dark head bent close to Molly's smaller one. For a moment, Becca imagined them a family here, cooking dinner at night, helping Molly with her homework, cuddled on the sofa in front of the television.

She pushed the mental image away. Those kinds of dreams were too distracting right now.

The three of them worked in camaraderie for half an hour then the aroma of fresh-baked cookies began to fill the air. Molly claimed the first cookie, and her face was soon smeared with chocolate. Becca had the next one and pronounced it perfect, if a little overdone.

She was conscious of Max's smiling gaze on her. Oh, how she wanted to believe the expression in his eyes.

"What did you do all morning?" Max asked.

"I finished Gram's accounting," Becca said. "It was quite a mess. I'm not sure she even knew how much money she had in the various accounts."

"She's a smart one. I imagine she knows what she's got."

"Maybe." Becca decided not to mention to Max how Gram had seemed upset. She wished she dared ask about the letter from Laura.

Molly took a tray of cookies and milk up to Gram's room, and Max hopped up and sat on the counter. "Today I realized I want what you have, Becca."

"What's that?"

His face reddened. "A relationship with God. Molly needs Him, too."

Becca's heart gave a leap of joy. "Max, that's wonderful!"

"I'd been thinking about it when we first moved here and I got to know Gram and her faith. I saw something I wanted. But when Laura died—" He shrugged. "I guess I blamed God. But thanks to you, I'm seeing how much I'm missing. And how much Molly is missing."

This seemed proof that he couldn't have tried to hurt her last week. Becca smiled so much her face hurt. "Want me to call the pastor?"

"I already did. Molly and I stopped by to see him on the way home. He prayed with me and I know God was just waiting to welcome me home like the prodigal son. I'm ready to face life again."

She couldn't speak, her heart was too full. God had answered her prayers.

He squeezed her fingers. "How about we make a date for the island picnic on Saturday?"

She'd heard about the picnic. There would be log-rolling contests and bake-offs as well as tree-climbing and log-cutting just like in the old days. "Okay."

She just wished she could rid herself of the last niggling doubts she had about Max.

The phone rang, and he answered it. "It's for you," he said, handing her the phone.

Jake's deep voice gladdened her heart even more. "Ready for some company?" he asked. "Wynne and I will be there tomorrow."

Chapter Eighteen

Becca stood on the pier and watched the distant boat draw closer. Behind her, the rest of the family waited also. She felt she would have real allies once her siblings were here.

"I have all kinds of new cousins," Molly said. "Why is your sister named Wynne? I never heard that name before."

"It's an old Southern name," Becca told her. "She was named for my mother's sister. You'll like her. She loves kids. I imagine she'll have half a dozen of them when she gets married."

The specks on the boat deck came into view, and she saw Wynne and Jake wave. A lump grew in her throat, and she waved back frantically. The sound of the engine grew closer then Jake tossed a rope toward the dock, and Max caught it. He tied it to the dock post and pulled the boat in tight to the pier.

"Becca!" Wynne leaped from the deck and engulfed her in a stranglehold.

Hugging her sister's tiny frame gave Becca a burst

of intense joy. "I've missed you so much!" She held Wynne at arm's length. "You're tanned."

Wynne looked fabulous. Her silky black hair hung over one shoulder in a French braid, and her amber-brown eyes shone with enthusiasm and confidence. Wynne had never heard the word *can't* and her take-charge attitude didn't fit her five-foot-three slender frame. She might look slight and insignificant, but Becca knew her sister's sheer force of personality carried her to success in whatever she did.

"Hey, it's my turn." Jake grabbed Becca and lifted her in a bear hug. "How's my baby sister?"

Though Becca stood nearly eye level with Jake, he outweighed her by eighty pounds. Muscular and stocky, he would have fit in with their lumberjack ancestors. His black hair fell over one dark eye in a rakish way that made him look younger than his thirty years. His massive hands spanned her waist, but Becca had seen those same hands brush dirt tenderly away from delicate fossils.

"Hey, what's that on your neck?" Wynne asked, peering up at Becca.

Becca covered her neck with her hand. "Nothing."

"Let me see." Jake pulled her hand away. "Who choked you?" He turned and glared at the assembled group waiting to be introduced on the pier.

"Take it easy." Showing no fear of her brother, Max stepped forward and put out his hand. "Welcome to Eagle Island. I'm Max Duncan."

Jake hesitated then shook hands. "What's going on here?"

"Someone tried to kill Becca last week," Max said. "She's fine, but I'm glad you're here. We need to guard her."

Wynne gasped and turned to Becca. "You're leaving here. Now."

"I'm fine. The sheriff is on top of it." Trust Wynne to notice every little thing.

Jake's keen eyes scanned the group and lingered on his grandmother.

Gram came forward, holding out her hand. "Hello, Jake. Come give your grandmother a hug."

His face softened, and he bent and embraced her. "Hi, foxy lady."

"Ah, Jake, still the same impertinent boy," Gram said with evident satisfaction. "No one has called me that since you were here last."

"Why does he call her that?" Shayna wanted to know. She stepped forward and gave Jake a sultry smile.

"Charles used to call me that, and Jake thought it great fun to tease." Gram hugged Jake again before releasing him and reaching for Wynne. "Wynne, darling, you are still so tiny. You never did grow."

"Good things come in small packages," Wynne said as she embraced Gram. "Oh, good, you still wear the lilac scent. I used to dream about that when I was missing you."

Tears filled Gram's eyes. "You missed me?"

Wynne nodded. "I used to cry and beg my parents to let me come visit." She bit her lip, and her eyes grew luminous with tears.

Becca had forgotten how attached Wynne had been to Gram. She remembered the tantrums the first summer they didn't come. Wynne had screamed that Mom hated her. It had taken three summers for her to quit nagging about it.

Watching them now, she noticed how much Wynne

looked like Gram. They had the same small build, though Gram was portly with age now.

Becca wondered if there were any pictures of Gram when she was a girl. She'd have to look in the attic.

Gram was wiping her eyes, and so was Wynne. "You're here now," Gram said. "And you'll be welcome here any time, always. You all know that."

Wynne whirled in a flurry of motion. "I'm back on Eagle Island!" she screamed.

Jake shook his head. "You see what I put up with, Gram? Between a career student and Wynne in a manic state, I'm lucky to remember my own name."

"Oh, hush, Jake, you're as tickled to be here as the rest of us." Wynne glanced at the rest of the group. "Okay, introduce everyone."

"You don't remember your cousin Tate?" Tate slung an arm around Wynne's shoulders. "I tossed you out of the barn into the hay wagon one summer, remember?"

"And you nearly drowned me the summer you tried to teach me how to swim," Wynne said.

"I'd forgotten about that," Tate admitted. "And this lovely woman is my wife, Shayna."

"You poor girl," Wynne said. Her gaze lingered on Nick. "And who's this gorgeous man?"

Nick's smile widened, but Shayna looked as though she'd like to claw Wynne's eyes out.

"This is my brother, Nick," Max said. "And this is my daughter, Molly." He pulled Molly forward.

Wynne smiled and knelt in front of Molly. "I bet you know all the best places on the island already, don't you?"

"You're sure pretty," Molly said.

"I agree," Nick said. He was staring at Wynne as if she was the most luscious hot fudge sundae ever made.

Becca was thankful she hadn't been taken in by his smooth ways. Her gaze sought and found Max. He was looking at her, not Wynne, and the smile on his face made her cheeks grow warm.

"Let's all move inside," Gram said. "Moxie will have tea and coffee ready for you."

"And Daddy and me made chocolate chip cookies yesterday," Molly said, slipping her hand into Wynne's. "Becca helped, too, but I did most of it."

"I'm sure they're delicious, too," Wynne said.

Becca lagged behind as the rest trooped inside. Max turned and came back to where she lingered.

"I can see why you were eager for them to get here. You've got allies. Or I should say *we* have allies. I feel better knowing there are two more people we know we can trust to look out for you."

"I feel like a huge boulder has been rolled off my shoulders," Becca admitted.

They spent the next few days exploring and getting caught up on news. On Saturday, they all piled in cars and headed out to Windigo Park, a bird preserve that still boasted some of the last native birch and sycamore stands in North America. Loggers from the mainland had been pouring in for the last few days to take part in the festivities.

Red-and-yellow banners flew from atop tall pines to mark the parking areas. Becca craned her neck to look around.

"What kind of contests are you entering?" she asked Max.

"Log-rolling, ax throw, two-man crosscut," he said. "And I might try my hand at the pole-climbing." He nodded toward two giant pine poles that seemed to go up high enough to touch the sky.

"Oh," she breathed. "It looks dangerous."

"I'll be fine. I've done this for years." He parked and jumped out, hurrying around to the trunk where he pulled out a satchel with his gear.

People were hurrying everywhere. Becca saw Wynne go off with Nick while Jake ushered Gram toward the refreshment tent. The aroma of barbecued beef wafted through the air, and women carried home-made desserts and casseroles toward the tables outside the tent.

Becca grabbed the corn casserole she'd made from the backseat and followed Max.

"Stay close," he instructed. "I'm not so sure you should have come to this today. Accidents can happen too easily at things like this. I should ask Jake to make sure he stays close by you while I'm competing."

"Are you kidding?" Becca nodded toward her brother. "He's signing up to compete."

Jake was signing the contestant form. Max grinned. "He's strong enough to be a contender. Has he ever done anything like this before?"

"No, but that's never stopped him." She looked around for Shayna and Tate, but they had disappeared into the crowd. She saw her friend Saija and waved.

Saija hurried to join them and smiled down at Molly. "Hey, sweetie, I was hoping you were going to be here. The rest of the kids are in the junior lumberjack area. You want me to show you where to go?"

"Yeah!" Molly scampered off with Saija.

"I'm going with them," Becca told Max. He nodded, and she hurried after them. "Saija, wait!"

Saija stopped and pointed out the junior lumberjack group to Molly who ran to join the rest of the children.

Becca grabbed Saija's arm and leaned in to whisper to her. "I want to talk to Greg."

"Why?"

"He's a fisherman. I just wondered if he could have seen something the day my parents died." She stared into Saija's face. "Don't tell Max, though. He'll try to stop me. He thinks Greg would do anything to make me suspicious of him."

"I think I know where he is, but I'm not sure Greg can help you." Saija led Becca through the forest toward the sound of chain saws. They found Greg standing at the edge of the clearing where the contestants were preparing for the one-man log-cutting contest.

He saw them, and his eyes widened. "You're off your leash?" he asked with a sneer.

"No leash." She gave him a friendly smile hoping to defuse the anger she sensed still bubbling under the surface. "I was looking for you."

"For me? Lover boy is apt to be mad."

"I wanted to ask you if you've heard anything in the village about my parents' accident. Any rumors of what could have happened and why. Or if maybe you saw something out on the water that day."

"Would you believe me if I told you?"

"I'd listen." She gazed into his face with as much candor as she could muster.

He shrugged. "I've heard Robert Jeffries might have had something to do with it."

"Robert Jeffries! Mrs. Jeffries's son?" She'd expected him to rail against Max and that she'd have to weed through his accusations to find anything helpful.

To have him toss such a choice tidbit out without a fight made her fumble for what to say.

"Yeah. He thought he was going to get a cut of the estate when the old lady passed on. When your dad arrived, he told your grandmother that she'd done enough for the Jeffries family; she shouldn't be giving them more Baxter money. Your grandmother called a lawyer and was going to cut Robert out of the will."

"How do you know all this?"

"My sister's friend worked for the attorney."

"But why would he kill them if he was already out of the will?"

"Revenge, I guess." Greg shrugged.

"He showed up one day shortly after I arrived. He acted like he owned the house. Why would Gram put him in the will in the first place? And how would he know who I was? Someone tried to kill me the day I arrived."

"Maybe he recognized you."

"Maybe." Still unconvinced, she chewed on her lip. Robert's guilt sounded too easy.

"Rumor has it that he might be your dad's by-blow. Maybe he was trying to eliminate all the heirs, one by one."

Becca gasped. "You're lying," she whispered.

He grinned. "I just wanted to see if you were listening. I was just kidding."

"Some joke."

"Sorry." He didn't look penitent. "It shouldn't affect you since you wouldn't be related to him. I presume you've heard the truth of your own parentage."

"It's not the truth!" He seemed to be enjoying rattling her too much, and she wanted to slap him. Her parents weren't the people she thought they were. All her life they'd preached to her about living her life in a transparent way so people could see Christ through her. To find out they had all these secrets in their past was nearly enough to rattle her own faith.

He just shrugged. "I know it for a fact, Becca."

She froze. She'd asked God to show her the truth, but now she wasn't sure she wanted to face it. Maybe he was lying again. "How could you know the truth?"

"I overheard your mom talking to Will," he said simply. "I was ten years old and playing in the folly. She told him she was going to have his baby but that he could never tell Mason."

Becca's throat closed, and she couldn't utter a word. A cry fought to be heard, but all that finally emerged was a squeak. "No."

"Sorry, but it's the truth." He shrugged.

She thought she saw actual sympathy in his face. And there was no mistaking the honesty shining in his eyes. He was telling the truth. Her legs felt weak, and she sat on a stump. "I see."

"Sorry to have to tell you this, but you deserve to know the truth."

Becca couldn't take it all in. She wouldn't think about this now. "And Robert?" she asked.

"You mean why your grandmother put him in the will?" He shrugged. "You'll have to ask your grandmother."

"I will." Should she tell her grandmother the truth? Becca knew the rest of the family would see it as her trying to ensure her position. Gram deserved to know the truth though.

Greg turned toward the clearing as a man with a

bullhorn announced the beginning of a game. "I have to go." He walked away with a cocky strut.

Becca sighed and passed a hand over her face. "What am I going to do?" she whispered to Saija.

"You can't believe everything he says," Saija said. "He likes to stir up trouble."

"I think he was telling the truth." Becca took a deep breath. "I can't think about this now. Let's focus on my parents' murder. I wonder if Robert is here?"

"He's here. I saw him at the refreshment tent."

"I need to talk to Jake about this. Or Max. I'm so mixed up about this. I hate to do it alone."

"I'll come with you," Saija offered.

"Okay, great. Let's go find him."

The women wandered through the crowd but found no sign of Robert Jeffries. Becca paused to watch Max take on Jake and some other men in the pole-climbing contest. She cheered when Max won. Jake came in fourth, which wasn't bad for someone who had never competed before. The excitement of the contest kept the sick feeling in her stomach at bay.

She wasn't her father's daughter. The thought kept pounding through her brain in a litany that nearly drove her mad. She had a feeling this confirmation would change things in ways she couldn't imagine.

Becca snagged a bottle of water from an iced tub near the refreshment tent then left Saija talking to another woman. A path led from the clearing toward a clear stream that ran toward Lake Superior. Becca followed the path to a small cabin.

The sounds of laughter and shouting seemed distant here with the birds chirping above her head and the sound of the gurgling brook.

"I heard you were looking for me."

Becca jerked around and faced Robert Jeffries. "Who told you that?"

"Greg Chambers." He strolled into the clearing. An ax dangled from his hand.

"Have you been competing?"

He shook his head. "Not yet. The ax-throwing contest won't be for another half an hour. Long enough for me to practice." He raised his arm and threw the ax toward her; its head plowed into the log she was sitting on.

She yelped and sprang to her feet as wood chips flew into her face. The blood drained from her head and she felt faint. "You could have killed me," she whispered. She stared at the ax.

He laughed. "If I had wanted to hurt you, you'd be dead," he sneered. He advanced farther into the clearing and propped his leg on the log. "What do you want with me?"

She might as well blurt it out. Maybe the shock would make him reveal something. "I want to know if you killed my parents."

His eyes widened, then he grinned. "Like I'd tell you if I did. But no, it wasn't me. You should ask lover boy."

"Max? He had nothing to do with it."

"Yeah, that's what he'd like you to believe. How much will you pay me if I get the goods on him?"

"What goods?"

"I bet I could get proof that he sabotaged the boat just like he did his wife's. Honey, you don't have good judgment in men. You'd better watch your back if you marry him."

Becca felt the stirrings of panic. What was she doing in this deserted clearing with Robert Jeffries? She must be nuts. She sidled toward the path that led back to people. "I'd better get going."

Robert grabbed her arm. "No, you don't. Not until we come to an agreement. Fifty thousand dollars and you'll have the proof you need to hang Max Duncan."

Max stepped from behind a tree. "I was looking for you, Becca."

Becca's heart sank at the coldness in his voice. "Max, I—I was asking Robert some questions."

"So I heard." His face was like granite as he looked at her.

She couldn't bear the disappointment she glimpsed in his eyes. "It's not like it sounded. I wasn't fishing for information about you."

"That's not what I heard." He grabbed her elbow and ushered her toward the path.

"You're history now, Duncan." Robert's voice brayed after them. "You'd better be looking for a new home."

"Max—"

"Later." His clipped voice cut her off.

"I heard he might—"

"I thought you trusted me, Becca. Was it just a ruse to get past my defenses? All this time you thought I killed your parents, is that it? And you still think I tried to kill you the other night, I suppose." He sounded suddenly weary.

"No, Max, that's not it! Would you listen to me?" Becca grabbed his shoulders and shook him. "You are so pigheaded." She grabbed his head and kissed him. "There. Does that convince you? I love you, okay? You stupid, impossible man. I love you. I heard that Robert sabotaged the boat, not you. I was asking him about that."

Max shook his head as though dazed. He kissed her before she could say anything more. "Say it again," he murmured.

"I love you," she whispered against his lips. "I knew you didn't have anything to do with it. Robert just offered to give me proof for fifty thousand dollars. I knew he was just blowing smoke."

Max clutched her so close she couldn't breathe. "Okay, I believe you," he said.

She burrowed against his chest. "Now that we have that settled, don't you have something to say to me?"

He grinned. "I might. But you're going to have to wait. I've got to go cut down a tree."

"Oh, you're impossible!" She scurried along beside him as he walked toward the group of men milling around waiting for the contest to start.

Becca felt so happy she could burst as she watched Max throw himself into the contest. She was grinning like an idiot, she knew.

She felt the back of her neck prickle and turned to see Robert staring intently at her. His narrowed eyes and tight mouth made her shudder. He gave her a small salute then melted into the crowd.

Chapter Nineteen

After the excitement of the lumberjack contests yesterday, Max had rushed through his shower to see Becca. Now sitting with her in church, he felt complete and whole. Molly held his hand on his left, and he glanced at Becca from the corner of his eye.

She looked so beautiful with the sunshine sparkling through the stained-glass window and shimmering on her hair. A burgeoning happiness filled him so full he thought he couldn't contain it.

He drank in the words of the sermon. Since he'd prayed with the minister, life seemed bright with promise. Becca's coming had changed everything. God knew what he needed before Max had realized it.

When was the last time he'd felt this eager and happy? Years ago, he knew. Maybe never. He tried to remember how life had been with Laura, but too many awkward and unhappy moments blurred his memory of the early days.

After church, he held Becca's hand as they walked to the car. The same happiness shone on her face that he knew was on his. He was almost afraid to talk about the future for fear this joy would vanish if he looked at it too closely.

The next morning, his mood was still simmering on high. Max had enough time to look through some business affairs before breakfast. He whistled as he turned on his computer. Glancing at his watch, he saw he had time to order supplies for the next month. Though it was nearly nine o'clock, the house was quiet. Gram and Molly had gone for a walk to the folly. Molly was always thrilled when she got Gram to herself. Jake and Wynne had gone to town, and Tate, Nick and Shayna weren't up yet.

The grandfather clock in the hall ticked loudly in the silence of the house. He went to Gram's office and rummaged through the desk for the number of the store on the mainland. Everything was much more orderly now that Becca had worked her magic.

She'd been good for all of them. He smiled tenderly at the thought. She'd changed his life, his and Molly's and Gram's.

The household checkbook was in the lap drawer. He pulled it out and flipped it open to see if he needed to transfer funds to cover the purchase he intended to make. Only two hundred dollars, he'd better transfer some money. He got out the savings book and opened it.

His eyes widened at the figure at the bottom. It was over two hundred and fifty thousand dollars less than he'd expected. Where had it gone? The entries listed didn't add up to the final total. A final total in Becca's handwriting had a notation to the side that said Adjustment.

He pulled the phone toward him and dialed the bank. After being transferred to accounting, he explained the discrepancy.

"We show several transferals of fifty thousand dollars to a Rebecca Lynn Baxter's account," the woman told him. "Is there a problem, Mr. Duncan?"

"Would you fax me the details of those transactions, please?" he said. This couldn't be true. Becca wouldn't do something like this. Embezzle from her own grandmother? It didn't make sense.

He hung up the phone and put it down. Surely there was some explanation. Could Gram have asked Becca to do this? Or maybe Gram herself had done it.

All his questions about Becca came surging back. Had she come here to get close to her grandmother for money? She'd been in school awhile and maybe she had large education bills to pay. Gram would have been more than happy to help with that.

He shook his head. Not two hundred and fifty thousand dollars worth of school bills. He was grasping at straws because he didn't want to believe the evidence. Becca seemed so pure and innocent, but he'd been burned before. Laura had pulled the wool over his eyes, too. It looked like he didn't have good judgment when it came to women. He looked at the exterior and didn't see the corruption under the pretty skin and soft eyes.

The fax machine began to spit out pages, and he glanced at the first one then laid it down again. What a mess he was. He'd never been in a single good relationship in his life. Why did he think this one would be any different? He should have known better.

He heard footsteps in the hall, and his stomach tightened. The coming confrontation wouldn't be pleasant.

"Good morning." Becca smiled at him from the doorway.

"Hi." He couldn't bear to look in her face. Such seemingly innocent eyes and smile. "Could I talk to you for a minute?"

"Sure, what's up?"

He dared a glance at her. Wariness had replaced the open love on her face. That hurt, but what he had to say would likely keep that expression of devotion from ever crossing her face again.

"I wonder if you can explain this?" He walked to the fax and picked up the papers the bank had faxed over.

She took one of them from his fingers and read it over. "Transferred to my account? This makes no sense." Her brow creased with a frown that deepened when she met his gaze. "You—you don't think I did it, do you?"

When he didn't answer, she thrust it back at him. "Ask Gram if she had anything to do with it."

"There's more." He handed the faxed pages to her. "Four transfers in all, Becca—one a week. All into your account. Did you think you could just bleed Gram dry and no one would notice?"

"I didn't do it, Max." She met his gaze.

How did she do it—how did she manage to look so innocent when the truth was staring them both in the face? "Becca, you must admit it looks bad."

"If you loved me, you wouldn't be so quick to jump to the conclusion I'm guilty," she said quietly. "But you never did say it yesterday, did you? Was it just a ploy to get my guard down so you could accuse me of theft?"

"I don't want to believe it," he said. "Help me understand. Did you need the money for something important?"

"I didn't take it, Max, but it looks as though it's going to be impossible to convince you of that."

Her eyes seemed enormous, luminous and shimmering. If she cried, he was going to turn tail and run. "How did the money get in your account if you didn't do it? Who besides yourself would know your account number?"

He heard the desperation in his voice. Surely she had to realize he wanted to believe her. If she could just give him some reasonable explanation, he'd grab it with both hands. "That money didn't just magically appear in your bank account."

"I realize that. Someone obviously is trying to make me look bad. And succeeding." She balled the papers up and tossed them at him. "Here, you figure it out. I don't want to talk to you about this anymore. I'm wasting my time when it's clear you think I'm a liar and a cheat."

"I'm going to have to talk to Gram about this."

"Of course you are," she said bitterly. "You've been looking for a weakness you could exploit, haven't you? What a bonanza. Did you move the money yourself, Max?"

He didn't give her question the dignity of an answer. "I want you to move the money back to Gram's account."

"With pleasure." She dropped her purse from her shoulder and rummaged through it before drawing out her checkbook. She stalked to the phone and dialed with jerky movements.

"I'd like to transfer some money," she said. She read off the account number, then her face paled. "Are you sure?" she whispered. She listened a few moments.

"Could you fax me over the last ten transactions?" She rattled off the fax number then hung up the phone.

"Don't tell me. The money's gone." He should have known she'd pull something like this. She wouldn't want the money left where it could be retrieved.

Her face was nearly as white as the lace curtains at the window. She wet her lips. "I'm actually overdrawn by fifty dollars. They used my overdraft protection."

"Where was it transferred to?"

"A Swiss bank account." Her blue eyes searched his face. "I know how this looks, Max. Don't you think I'd be smarter than to pull something like this?"

"You weren't expecting to get ~~caught~~," he said. "With doing Gram's accounting yourself, you had no idea anyone would take a close look at the accounts. It was just a fluke I noticed the discrepancy."

The front door opened, and he heard the sound of Gram and Molly's laughter.

"You run along and go potty," Gram said. "When you get back, we'll have some tea."

"Okay." Molly's steps raced past the office.

Max waited until he heard her on the steps then went to the doorway. "Gram, would you come in here please?"

Becca paled even further, so much so that he wondered if she might faint.

"Is something wrong, Max?" Gram evidently heard the solemn note in his voice.

"Unfortunately, yes." He pointed to the desk chair. "You'd better have a seat."

Gram shot him a puzzled look but did as he said. "Becca, are you all right? You look as though you're about to fall over. Come sit by me."

"I'm fine, Gram," Becca whispered.

"Gram, some money has turned up missing from your savings account. Two hundred and fifty thousand dollars."

"I know," Gram said. "Becca told me the account balances, and I realized something was wrong. Do I need to cash in some stock or break into a certificate of deposit?"

"No, you have enough liquid money for now. That's not the most immediate problem." Max wasn't sure her heart could take the stress of what he had to tell her. "Why didn't you tell me when you heard about it?"

"Tell me and quit beating around the bush, Max. I'm too old to play games."

"He thinks I took it, Gram," Becca burst out.

"Oh, is that all? You know you can have whatever you need, Becca. Do you need more?"

"I didn't take it, Gram." Becca was beginning to sound even more desperate.

"Did you hear her, Max? She didn't take it."

"It was transferred to her account, Gram. And from there to a Swiss bank account."

"I see." Gram fell silent a few moments. "Who could have done this, Becca? If you say you had nothing to do with it, I believe you."

"I know, Gram. You understand love, unlike other people."

Max ran his hand through his hair. "What am I supposed to think, Becca? The evidence is right here in black and white!" He grabbed up a handful of papers and shook them in the air.

"Max, that's no way to talk to Becca."

Gram's rebuke stung. "And this was no way for her to treat the grandmother she says she loves."

"Someone else has done this to implicate her," Gram said.

"It must be nice to live in a dreamworld."

The fax machine whirred to life and spat out some pages. He stalked to the machine and grabbed up the papers.

"Let me see," Becca said. She peered over his shoulder.

There were five large deposits and only one recent withdrawal. The Swiss number meant nothing to him. Except the end of a dream he should have known better than to harbor.

Becca felt battered and bruised. It felt like years ago that Max had looked at her with love in his eyes. And it hadn't been love, obviously. It had been a chimera, a mirage. If this was what love felt like, she never wanted to go through it again.

She wouldn't have believed Max could turn so fast from the tender, caring man she'd come to love into this cold-eyed man who refused to listen to her explanations.

"We already know someone here hates me," she said. "Someone has tried to kill me several times. And someone killed my parents."

"I don't know what to believe anymore," Max said. "Have all of the so-called attempts on your life been ruses meant to throw us off the trail of why you're really here?"

"Max, that's enough!" Gram rose. "You're upsetting Becca."

Becca felt she would explode if she stayed in this room another minute. She couldn't bear to see the accusation in his eyes. "I'm going for a walk," she said.

She didn't wait for an answer but turned and raced for the door.

"Becca, wait!" her grandmother called after her.

She didn't want to upset her grandmother, but she couldn't talk. Her throat was too tight. She flung open the front door and dashed outside. Her heart raced inside her tight chest. She wanted off this island and away from Max Duncan and his accusatory gaze.

Running around the side of the house, she almost knocked Shayna down. Becca put out her hands to catch her. "Sorry," she said.

"Where are you going in such a hurry?" Shayna glanced into Becca's face.

"Anywhere as long as it's away from Max." Becca was in no mood to talk. She veered around Shayna in angry strides and walked toward the back of the house.

"Hey, you okay?" Shayna called after her.

Becca just raised her hand in the air and kept on walking. The last thing she wanted was to explain to another person that the man she loved thought she was a thief and a liar.

Tears burned her eyes, and her vision blurred. *Oh, God, why? I can't stand this. Hold me, Lord. Help me to cling to you right now.*

She jogged through the garden and into the trees, plunging through the brush past the tree house and toward the folly. Whips of brush caught in her hair and sprang toward her face, but she pushed them out of the way and kept on going.

She broke free of the tree line and stopped in the rubble around the folly. The crumbling building loomed in front of her. She remembered Tate's furtive trip there a few weeks ago. Maybe now would be a good time to explore the old ruin. It would get her mind off her troubles.

She glanced around. Not an animal moved. The wind

sighed through the treetops, but not even birds chirped here. She'd often wondered why this place was so still, almost as though it were cursed.

Climbing over the shale and shattered brick, she wandered through the ruins, remembering the fun she had playing here as a child. She finally gained the slope to the front door and stood in front of it, half afraid to go in. The building probably wasn't safe, but at this moment, she really didn't care.

Squaring her shoulders, she pushed the half-ajar door fully open. A startled bird fluttered past her cheek, and she flinched, then watched it fly through a gaping hole in the roof. Debris littered the floor, old papers, crumpled brick and plaster, slate tiles from the decayed roof and animal droppings.

It wasn't the fairy-tale place of her memory. Why would Tate have come in here? She picked her way through refuse to the room at the far end. The door hung open and she nudged it with her foot until it squeaked back against the wall. The small room that met her gaze was even more disreputable than the first. She stepped inside and looked around. She would have sworn there was once another room here.

She wiped her hand over her face and leaned against the wall. Becca felt something shift, then the wall began to fall away from her. She reached out to try to stop her fall but grasped only air. Flailing, she fell backward on top of the crumbling wall and tumbled into a space the broken rubble revealed.

She landed hard. The wind had been knocked out of her, and she struggled to catch her breath. At least she hadn't broken anything. She lurched to her feet and turned to survey the room.

Someone had cleaned in here. The floor was swept, and a bed sat in the middle of the room. Covered with a clean quilt and pillows, it looked comfy and inviting. But how had anyone gotten in here? She glanced around but could see no other way in or out. Maybe there was a hidden door somewhere.

Someone had been living here. An old wardrobe was the only piece of furniture in the small cubicle other than the bed. She walked over to it and opened the oblong door.

A huge headdress of feathers, bone and teeth hung from a hook inside. Becca remembered the figure in the woods that had tried to kill her and flinched back, not wanting to even touch the thing.

Tate? She felt cold. She never would have suspected him.

She couldn't bear to look at the hideous thing. She shut the doors. Two drawers were below. She pulled open the first drawer and found a shoe box inside. She pulled it out and opened the lid.

Inside was a mishmash of pictures and papers. Rummaging through them, she found one of her parents when they'd first been married. They looked so young and utterly happy. Her mother was staring up at her father with an adoring expression that brought a lump to her throat. No matter what anyone said, she found it impossible to believe her mother could have betrayed her father.

She sat on the edge of the bed and began to look through the papers. They looked like old love letters from her parents to one another. The missives were tattered and yellow with age.

She read several, smiling at the sentiment in them.

Her father had been quite eloquent, more than she would have imagined. About halfway down, she opened a newer letter written on stationery that still held a hint of perfume. She didn't recognize the handwriting.

Nick. We have to move quickly. Meet me at our spot tonight at midnight. Be ready for anything. Our future hinges on what we must do tonight.
Shayna

Nick and Shayna. Why had she never seen it before? Shayna's jealousy when Nick had shown too much attention to other women had seemed merely that of a beautiful woman piqued at attention paid to another.

Becca reread the note. What did they have to move quickly on? The note was too cryptic to understand but still ominous. Maybe there was more in the box. She rummaged through more love letters then found the same stationery near the bottom of the box.

Nick. We have one more obstacle in our way. I've been going through pictures for that scrapbook for Gram, and I recognized Rebecca when we were introduced. We have to make sure Gram never realizes who she is. I've destroyed the letter from Will to Suzanne that proves she's Will's child. And I have a plan. Meet me tonight.
Shayna

She *was* Will's child. Gram was right. She *was* the only child of Gram's oldest son. No wonder Nick and Shayna saw her as an obstacle. Gram was adamant about giving her the lion's share of the estate, just as she'd been determined to give Mason the same until he'd been killed.

Shayna must have thought Tate would still get the estate once Mason was out of the way, and then when Becca showed up, Shayna had suspected what Gram would do if it ever came to light that she was Will's child.

An envelope lay under the letter, and she pulled it out. An account book and a paper with access codes for a Swiss bank account. They'd taken Gram's money as well and tried to frame her with it.

It made sense. They knew the theft would be discovered, and Becca would be disgraced. Since, so far, they'd failed to kill her, she would be discredited.

She finally had the answers. Her parents had been murdered, and Shayna and Nick wanted her dead, as well. But something still didn't make sense. Why would Nick be involved? It was Tate who would get the lion's share if Becca were dead. She swallowed hard as she tried to figure it out.

Shayna wouldn't get the house or much of the estate if she divorced Tate and married Nick. Becca chewed on her lower lip. But would Shayna divorce him? If she'd murdered once, she might again. As Tate's widow, she would inherit all of it.

Though she had no proof, she knew she'd stumbled on the truth. Not only was her life in danger, but Tate's, as well. She heard a sound behind her and whirled.

"I see you found my little love nest." Nick stood smiling benignly in the doorway.

Becca jumped and put a hand over her thudding heart. The box dropped on the floor. She stooped to pick up the jumbled papers.

"Leave them." Nick's tone stayed amiable.

"How do you plan to kill Tate?" she blurted before she could stop herself.

Nick's smile faded. "What are you talking about?"

"It makes sense. You have nothing to gain with him still alive." Becca stood, glancing out of the corner of her eye for a weapon.

Nick casually pulled a small revolver from his pocket. "Don't move, Becca."

"Good, you got here in time." Shayna joined Nick in the doorway.

Two against one. Becca prayed for strength as she grabbed a broken stool and sprang toward them.

Chapter Twenty

"You were wrong, Max," Gram said.

The same thought had been going through Max's head for the past hour. He'd jumped to conclusions, and now that he'd had time to cool off, he knew the Becca he loved wouldn't have done what he'd assumed she did.

"I should go look for her," he said.

"You're finally saying something smart," Gram said. "Though I'm not sure she'll accept your apology."

"She has to." He went to the door and stepped outside. Where would she have gone? He walked along the edge of the water for a ways, but saw no sign of her. Retracing his footsteps, he checked the barn, but all the vehicles were inside except the one Jake and Wynne had taken.

After an hour of searching, he still couldn't find her. Jake and Wynne came home from town, and Max flagged them down. He explained what happened.

"Man, you are an idiot," Jake said. "A more honest person doesn't live than my sister."

"I know, I was wrong. I'm getting worried about her. She's been gone more than two hours."

"Let's fan out and look for her," Wynne said. She walked toward the back of the house while the men went along the water in opposite directions.

By midafternoon, Max was ready to call the sheriff. What if something had happened to Becca? The previous attempts on her life had been real, and she could be in terrible danger. He had to find her.

Becca wiggled her wrists experimentally. The rope holding her didn't budge. Nick had tied her so tightly, the bonds cut into the skin of her arms, and her hands ached. The cold from the hard ground seeped into her bones.

Her head hurt from where Nick had clubbed her with the gun when she tried to break past them. Her attack had been short-lived.

"They're looking for her," Shayna said. "We've got to get her out of here. Tate might think to look here."

"If he sobers up enough to think about it," Nick said with a sneer.

"What should we do with her?" Shayna asked.

"The easiest thing would be to take her out in the boat and toss her overboard. The cold would make short work of her and the fish wouldn't leave much left to tell how she died. If Max hasn't discovered the missing money, he will soon. They'll all think she couldn't live with the guilt of her crime."

"Good idea." Shayna peered through the window. "We don't dare wait until dark. They could come busting in here any minute."

"I'll bring the boat around to Fisherman's Cay on the

other side of the forest. It's only a fifteen-minute trek or so for you. Bring her around there in half an hour." He handed her the gun. "Use this if you have to."

Becca watched Shayna take the gun and check it. Maybe she had a chance. Shayna alone would be easier to take on. She prayed for strength and the right opportunity.

Nick kissed Shayna then disappeared into the other room, and moments later the door creaked and he was gone.

"You won't get away with this," Becca said. "My brother and sister will find me." She longed to say Max would be searching for her, but he would consider her death a blessing. The thought made her eyes burn.

"No one will suspect us," Shayna said. "After all, we have nothing to gain, right?" She smiled with obvious satisfaction. "We've been careful. Everyone thinks I've been mooning over Max." She giggled. "You swallowed my story without a problem."

She was right. Becca wiggled her wrists again when Shayna looked out the window then glanced at her watch.

"God sees what you're doing," Becca said.

Shayna's smile faded. "Shut up."

"You may get by with it in this life, but eternity is another matter."

"I said shut up!" Shayna stepped forward and slapped Becca across the mouth.

A trickle of warmth ran down from the corner of Becca's mouth, and she licked at it. It tasted coppery. "Don't do this, Shayna. No amount of money is worth murder," she pressed.

"You have no idea how much money Gram has, do you?"

"I don't care," Becca said.

"More fool you. She's got ten million in cash. The house and grounds are easily worth another five million."

"There would have been plenty for you without getting rid of me," Becca pointed out. "Gram intends to give Tate his share."

Shayna laughed. "I peeked at the will. A paltry million was all she planned to leave Tate. Molly, Jake and Wynne will get the same, and you'll get the rest. Tate was going to get the bulk of the estate until your parents showed up." She glanced at her watch again. "Time to go. You're about to meet God face-to-face."

"I'm not afraid, but you should be," Becca said.

Shayna scowled and jerked Becca to her feet. She shoved her toward the door, and Becca stumbled and fell.

"It's going to be hard to walk all tied up. Can you tie my hands in front instead of in back?"

"Nice try. Get moving." Shayna jerked her to her feet and shoved her again.

Becca walked slowly through the rubble. Once outside, she intended to run for the house and yell for all she was worth.

As if she read her mind, Shayna jerked her back. "Wait a minute." She whipped a scarf out of her pocket and stuffed it in Becca's mouth.

Becca tried to spit it out, but it was wedged too tightly. Despair tightened her chest, but she pushed it away. She could still run. Walking out into the forest, she glanced around for the best route.

The trees crowded in so thickly, it would be almost impossible to outrun Shayna. And the other woman kept a tight hand on Becca's arm.

Shayna marched her through the trees toward the little inlet that circled around the back of Windigo Manor's property. If Becca was going to break free, she needed to do it now.

She pretended to stumble then wrenched her arm from Shayna's grasp. Free of the restraining grip, she dashed back the way they'd come, zigzagging through the trees.

She heard Shayna shout then rush after her. Desperation gave wings to her feet, and the breath came harsh in her lungs. She thought she was gaining ground then she was tackled from behind.

Shayna's weight bore her to the ground, and the shock of hitting the unforgiving earth stole the breath from her lungs.

"Get up." The rage in Shayna's voice rendered her tone almost unrecognizable. "If you run again, I'll shoot you."

Becca recognized the deadly intent in the other woman's voice. Shayna dragged her to her feet and shoved her back toward the Cay. As they approached the beach, she heard the sound of a motor coming. Nick was at the helm of a small motorboat. He waved and guided the boat in close to shore.

Shayna yanked on Becca's arm again, and they both splashed into the water to the boat. The shock of Superior's icy water made Becca gasp.

"Cold, isn't it?" Shayna asked grimly. "The hypothermia will kill you in ten minutes."

Nick dragged her over the side of the boat, and she fell onto the bottom. He helped Shayna board the boat as well then revved up the motor and pointed the boat's bow toward the open water.

"Take her far out," Shayna hollered over the boat's motor.

Nick nodded. The cold spray struck Becca in the face. There was nowhere for her to go. If she jumped overboard, Superior's icy grip would just claim her sooner.

As she lay on the bottom of the boat, her necklace caught on an oar. She jerked her head to free it, but it broke instead and lay coiled on the bottom of the boat.

Fifteen minutes later Nick throttled back the motor. "This is as good a spot as any."

He reached in his pocket and pulled out a knife. The cold blade touched Becca's wrists then the bonds holding her fell away. Nick pulled her to her feet. "Sorry it has to end this way, Becca. I liked you."

"Get it over with," Shayna snapped.

For a minute Becca thought maybe Nick couldn't do it, then he shoved her. Caught off guard, she flailed to keep her balance, but it was no use, and she plunged overboard. The cold water closed over her head and nearly numbed her. She fought the water's icy grip, then her head broke the surface. She gasped in a breath.

"So long, Becca. It's been nice knowing you." Nick revved up the motor once again, and the boat zoomed away.

Becca wanted to shout after them, but she knew it was a waste of her lung power. She trod water a moment, praying for guidance. She wasn't done yet.

She glanced around at the horizon. Nothing but water. Then she spied a tiny glimpse of land to the north. Gull Island. She'd forgotten about the tiny speck of land. Unpopulated, it was hardly more than twenty feet in circumference. During rainy periods, it was totally submerged, but the summer had been dry. It might be her salvation.

She knew it was a long shot. The cold would kill her long before she ever reached it, but she had to try. Striking out strongly, she began to swim toward it. At first her movements were strong and sure, but the water's cold grip began to slow her down, make her sluggish. Her thoughts began to jumble as hypothermia dulled her senses.

Kick, stroke, kick.

She repeated the mantra to herself. It seemed she swam forever. The water kept breaking over her head as the cold tried to claim her. She struggled on, a faint prayer still echoing in her head. Her mouth and nose went under again, and she came up sputtering. Then her knees hit sand, and she realized the island was right in front her. A sandbar ran around the perimeter about a quarter of a mile from the actual shore.

The swim had to have taken at least half an hour. God had to have done this. She could never have made it on her own strength.

She stumbled to her feet and plodded through the shallow water toward land. Her teeth chattered, and she found it hard to think. It felt as if she walked forever before she reached the shelter of the trees. She sank to her knees. *"Thank you, Father,"* she whispered as she fell facedown into the sand.

When her senses came back to her more fully, she realized she was still in dire straits. There was no way to start a fire to warm herself, no one would think to look for her here. All she'd done was prolong her death.

No, she wouldn't think like that. God had brought

her this far. She had to keep going, had to find a way to get help.

The wind chilled her further, and she wrapped her arms around her. It had been years since she'd been on Gull Island, but if she remembered correctly, there was an old lean-to here somewhere. She stumbled to her feet and began to search in the fading light. It was nearly dark when she found what she was looking for.

It was not the cute little structure she remembered. Time had taken its toll, and the roof was gone as well as one of the walls. But a tattered blanket lay inside. Becca grabbed it up thankfully and shook the insects out of it then wrapped it around her shoulders. She wouldn't die just yet.

Max paced the living room carpet. The sheriff had left with his men to search, though Max and Becca's siblings had combed every inch of the island they could think to look. He rubbed his burning eyes.

Shayna handed him a cup of coffee. "Did you have a fight or anything?"

He hesitated.

"You did." Shayna shrugged her elegant shoulders. "When a woman is hurting, she does crazy things. Do you think she could have just decided to leave? That's what I would have done after a fight."

"Jake and Wynne are here. She wouldn't just go off and leave them without a word," he pointed out.

"What was the fight about?"

"Some of Gram's money is missing, and I was stupid enough to think for a minute that she took it," he admitted.

Shayna's eyes widened. "Could she have…committed suicide?"

Max froze. The thought had been playing at the edge of his mind for a few minutes, but to hear it spoken aloud made him feel sick. She wouldn't do something like that, would she? Becca was strong, and only cowards committed suicide.

"Something has happened to her," Wynne said. "Becca is the most thoughtful girl. She wouldn't have wanted to worry me and Jake like this. And she would never be so selfish as to try to kill herself. I'm afraid she's lying somewhere with a broken leg or something." She sounded near tears.

Jake slammed his fist onto the wall. "We have to find her."

"We can't do much tonight," Nick said. "It's too dark to see."

Though Max knew his brother was right, he couldn't bear the thought that Becca was out there somewhere hurt and alone. Maybe dead. The thought was like a splash of cold water. He couldn't believe that— wouldn't believe it.

"I'm going out again," he said abruptly.

"Me, too." Jake followed him.

The men split up again, and Max strode toward the cave where he'd found Becca once before. He called her name through the long night, praying all the while. But when dawn came, there was still no sign of Becca.

He watched the sun come up then went to the boat-house. Though he'd looked already, there was no boat missing. The small motorboat he often used bobbed in the water, and he was tempted to take it out onto the lake. He knew it was useless. If Becca was in the water, she was dead. But the urge wouldn't leave.

He went to the boat and got in. On the bottom he saw

something glitter and looked closer. Becca's necklace, the one with a small dolphin she always wore. He picked it up. What was it doing here? As far as he knew, she'd never taken this boat out.

He climbed out of the boat and went to the door of the boathouse. "Jake, Wynne, over here!" He saw them in the distance and waved.

Jake shouted back and he and his sister jogged toward Max. When they reached him, he showed them the necklace. "I'm going out on the lake," he said.

"We're going with you." Wynne dug her cell phone out and called the house to explain what they'd found. "Gram is calling the sheriff," she said when she hung up.

The three of them got in the boat, and Max fired up the engine. As they pulled away from the shore, he heard a shout and saw Nick trying to flag him down. "I'll be back soon!" he shouted back.

He raced the motor out into the water. Where to go? Lake Superior was huge. He tried to think of anyplace on it she could have gone where she would still be alive. That hope was fading with every minute. He prayed silently, asking for guidance.

God knew where she was. As suddenly as the thought came, he remembered Gull Island. It was a long shot, but what did he have to lose by checking there? He turned the bow of the boat in that direction.

The sun glimmered off the water as they rode the waves. Then the tiny island came into sight. He revved the engine higher, an urgency driving him on. The hull hit the sandy bottom a ways out from shore, and he tossed the anchor overboard.

"We'll have to walk from here." He cut the engine

and swung his legs overboard. Jake and Wynne followed him.

"I'd forgotten how cold the water was," Wynne gasped.

He dragged the boat more securely onto the sandbar, and they struck out for the land. Moments later they gained the sandy beach.

"Becca!" he shouted.

Jake and Wynne echoed his call. He tried not to think, tried not to face how ridiculous it was to think she might be here.

Then they heard an answering shout. Becca waved to them from down the beach.

"Becca!" Max felt a surge of joy and raced toward her. Jake and Wynne followed, but he reached her first and swept her into his arms.

Her hair hung in strands around her face, and she was shivering. He'd never seen a more beautiful sight. "Get a blanket from the boat," he shouted back to Jake. "There's one with the first-aid kit under the seat."

Becca's brother nodded and veered back the way he'd come. Max whipped off his jacket and slung it around Becca's shoulders.

"You found me. I prayed and prayed," Becca sobbed. She buried her face in his chest.

He clutched her tightly and kissed the top of her head. "I'm so sorry, Becca, so sorry. I was wrong and pigheaded. I love you so much. Don't ever scare me like that again."

Wynne reached them, and Becca turned to embrace her. The sisters clung together, both sobbing.

Jake arrived with the blanket and slung it around his sister. "What happened? How did you get out here?"

Becca hiccuped and pulled away from Wynne. "Nick and Shayna. They killed Mom and Dad."

Shock radiated through Max. "Nick? But why?"

"They want Gram's money. They plan to kill Tate once he has the lion's share. Then they can marry and live the life they want."

"They left you here?" Rage began to gather in Max's chest.

Becca shook her head. "They threw me into Superior. I remembered this island and decided to try to swim for it. God kept me going long enough to make it."

Max pulled her back against his chest, and his gaze met Jake's. "Call the sheriff," he said.

Becca held a cup of hot cocoa in her hands as she nestled against Max's side. He didn't want to let go of her. Molly curled against his other side, and Max had his arms around both his girls.

"Nick blabbed the whole plan when the sheriff arrested him," Max told her. He pressed his lips against her hair.

"I think it began as Shayna's idea," Becca said. She took a sip of cocoa and sighed in contentment. "She was tired of living on the island, but she didn't want to give up the chance of getting Gram's money."

"What about Gram's money that was missing?" Wynne asked.

"It was the backup plan since they hadn't managed to dispose of me. They wanted to discredit me so Gram would leave the money to Tate. Then they could kill Tate and have it all."

"And we have no way of getting it back for Gram," Jake said. "They'll never give us the account number."

Becca smiled. "The account book is in the folly. We can transfer it back."

"Are you going to be my mommy?" Molly asked, her hand patting Becca's face.

Becca's gaze grew shy, and she glanced up at Max then looked away.

Max's throat grew tight. He didn't deserve her after the way he'd treated her. "She is if I have any say in it." He wrapped a strand of her hair around his finger.

"Ask her, Daddy," Molly urged.

"Yeah, ask her," Jake said mockingly. His dark eyes gleamed with laughter.

Wynne punched him. "We should leave them alone for this," she said.

"Not on your life." Jake crossed his arms over his chest and leaned back in his chair.

"You wanting lessons for when you finally find someone crazy enough to marry you?" Max asked. He wanted to look at Becca, but he was suddenly scared. Maybe she didn't love him that way.

He finally dared to raise his gaze and look into Becca's blue eyes. The love he felt for her nearly silenced him. His breath whispered against her ear. "Marry me, Becca. I can't live without you."

"That's no way to propose," Jake scoffed. "You're supposed to get on your knees. And after what you've put her through, she deserves that much."

"Jake," Becca said threateningly. "Shut up."

He spread his hands. "I was just trying to help."

"Okay, fine." Max got up and knelt beside Becca. Before he could say anything, she put her hand over his lips then got down on the floor beside him.

"Don't you know by now never to listen to my brother? You don't have to grovel."

"I'd grovel gladly," he whispered as he took her in his arms. "You're the love of my life, Becca. Will you marry me?"

Becca put her hand over her mouth, and he could see it was all she could do not to burst into laughter. "Okay, but you have to promise never to listen to my brother again."

"Agreed," he said as his lips met hers.

* * * * *

Dear Reader,

I've always loved the old Gothic books with their creepy mansions and remote settings. *Windigo Twilight* has a lot of that flavor, and I love the location along Lake Superior in Michigan's Upper Peninsula. It's one of the last true wilderness areas in the Midwest and is like stepping back in time.

Since my lineage includes Blackfoot, Cree and Miami Indian, Native American myths have always fascinated me. The Ojibwa legends are particularly interesting, and I knew I had to write some of that lore into my stories. The result is my new suspense series, Great Lakes Legends. I hope you enjoy the excursion! Watch for the next two books in the series coming soon.

I love hearing from my readers. Visit me at www.colleencoble.com and e-mail me at colleen@colleencoble.com.

Colleen Rhoads

*And now, turn the page for a sneak preview of
Colleen Rhoads's next* GREAT LAKES
LEGENDS *tale, SHADOW BONES,
part of Steeple Hill's exciting new line,
Love Inspired Suspense!
On sale in November 2005
from Steeple Hill Books.*

Prologue

Wilson New Moon hummed as he walked through the meadow with his balsam airplane. He loved to watch it soar into the clouds. Sometimes he was tempted to throw it with all his might and see if it could reach heaven.

The preacher said God was in heaven, and Wilson was curious about that. Did God sit on a throne? Did he like balsam planes?

A big man, Wilson knew he wasn't smart like other men. He'd once heard a teacher say he'd always have the mental capacity of a twelve-year-old, but Wilson didn't think that was so bad. Twelve was practically an adult.

He loved this particular meadow in the springtime. Mushrooms would be popping up any day now. He could take what he found to the hunting shop in town and sell them for enough to buy material for more planes. This one was getting tattered, and The Sleeping Turtle in town needed more of his creations to sell.

He let the wind take the plane and shouted with exhilaration as it soared on the breeze. Capering in among the wildflowers, he screamed with the wind. He wished he could be a plane himself.

By the middle of the afternoon, he was exhausted. He tucked his plane under his arm. Maybe he should leave it here instead of hauling it to his cabin. Wilson had seen a cave around here somewhere. He scrabbled through the underbrush.

There it was. He uprooted a shrub and revealed the opening back into the mine. It was bigger than he remembered—big enough for him to explore.

Smiling hugely, he got on all fours and crawled inside. This could be his hidey-hole. He could play tricks on other mushroom hunters from here and scare them away.

He heard a sound, and his blood boomed in his ears. He looked behind him and saw a black face atop a figure dressed in black. White teeth bared, the creature reached for him.

A scream tore from his throat, and Wilson backpedaled as quickly as he could. It was *Asibikaashi,* the Spider Woman, weaver of dream catchers. Wilson had always feared her and her kind. Though the Ojibwa were encouraged to protect and revere her, he wanted nothing to do with anything that had eight legs.

The shriek that issued from his mouth hurt his ears. He turned and ran for his life. Every moment he expected to feel the silken thread of the Spider Woman's web entangle him and the sharp sting of her teeth entering his back. He didn't dare look behind him as he ran for safety.

Chapter One

"Mother, what were you thinking?" Skye Blackbird wanted to stamp her size-seven foot and proclaim this a hill she would die on. One look at her mother's face convinced her she'd be left bleeding on the hillside.

She felt like bursting into tears and fought the impulse with all her strength. This was her father's dream and her own that was about to vanish. Her mother had to listen to reason.

She jerkily tied a knot in the dream catcher on her lap, but not even keeping her hands busy kept her emotions from churning her stomach into knots.

Her shop, The Sleeping Turtle, was empty of customers this beautiful May morning. But even if tourists had packed the narrow aisles filled with herbs and Ojibwa paraphernalia, she wouldn't have been able to hold her tongue.

Skye's mother, Mary Metis, tucked one black lock behind her ear. "You're not being reasonable, Skye. Letting the man look for dinosaur bones won't hurt the running of the mine. I don't tell you how to operate your business, so don't tell me how to manage mine. I get enough of that from Peter." Her voice vibrated with a suppressed anger.

Skye hurried to smooth things over. "Are you mad at Peter? He's just trying to look out for you."

"I'm not a child."

"You're just ticked at him right now," Skye responded. "Peter has been good to you—to both of us. He always knows what's best."

"The mine belongs to me, not to you or Peter," her mother went on. "It's about time I started taking back some of the decision-making about it."

"But you don't even know these people," Skye protested. "We know nothing about them."

That wasn't exactly true, and she knew it. This paleontologist, Jake Baxter, was Mrs. Baxter's grandson. The Baxters had practically owned the entire island for years, though that knowledge did nothing to endear the man to Skye. She liked things to stay the same.

"We've known the Baxters for years," her mother said. "I don't understand your attitude. Jake Baxter merely wants to poke around a bit, see if he can dig up any bones."

Skye hadn't met Jake Baxter yet, but she already disliked him. "We've always been told some of the Old Ones are buried on our property. What if he disturbs their bones?"

"On *my* property," Mary said. She laid down a bundle of dried chives, tied with twine. The pungent odor permeated the shop and mingled with that of chamomile, comfrey, mint and other herbs.

"Okay, on your property. And besides, I've been running the garnet mine for you for the past four years. I think I should have some say. I can just see people swarming all over the place and disrupting the operation of the mine."

"He'll be on the slope, not actually in the mine," her mother pointed out.

Skye finally voiced her real objection. She didn't even want to think about it. "And what happens if he finds something important? He could close us down while he digs. Permanently! I'll never find the diamonds if that happens."

Her mother's face softened, and she reached out to touch Skye's face with gentle fingers. "Skye, there are no diamonds. Your father combed every inch of that mine searching and found nothing. I often think that disappointment was what drove him away."

Skye knew better. If she'd been a better daughter, her father wouldn't have left. If she could find the diamonds, maybe he'd hear of it and come back. "Please reconsider," she said in a low voice that quivered no matter how much she tried to keep it steady.

"Let it go, Skye. This is just for the summer. Jake will be gone before you know it." Mary fished a sheaf of herbs out of the basket by her feet and began to prepare another bundle.

"That's what he's telling you, but I have a bad feeling about this...."